THE MASTER OF KNOTS

Also By Massimo Carlotto

The Colombian Mule

THE MASTER OF KNOTS

Massimo Carlotto

Translated from the Italian by Christopher Woodall

ORION

First published in Great Britain in 2004 by Orion,
an imprint of the Orion Publishing Group Ltd.

© Copyright 2002 by Edizioni e/o
Via Camozzi, 1–00195 Roma
Original Italian title: Il Maestro di Nodi

Translation copyright © Christopher Woodall 2004

A CIP catalogue record for this book is available from the British Library.

ISBN 075285735 5 (hardback), 075286814 4 (trade paperback)

Typeset by Deltatype Ltd,
Birkenhead, Merseyside

Set in Adobe Garamond

Printed in Great Britain by
Clays Ltd, St Ives plc

The Orion Publishing Group Ltd
Orion House
5 Upper Saint Martin's Lane
London WC2H 9EA

For Horst Fantazzini

PROLOGUE

*T*he click of a switch and the dull hum of a hairdryer. Then a stream of hot air and the touch of a brush on sweat-soaked hair. He wanted her to continue looking impeccable. That was the word he had used. For him, everything had to be impeccable. He took care to dab away the saliva that drained from the corners of her mouth, held gaping by a hard rubber ball. A dog's ball.

His cruelty, too, was impeccable. He left no marks on her body, though at times the pain he inflicted was unbearable. But he also knew how to make her come: she had already had two orgasms since the start of their 'session'. That was his word. All her life she had yearned for such an expert dominator and this idea was the only thing that stopped her thinking about death.

He was going to kill her; she was sure of it. Yet she still couldn't quite imagine how. He was in no hurry, and meted out pain with slow, studied movements. Using a system of pulleys, he kept altering her position and with each new move the power of his playful imagination astounded her.

He removed her blindfold and ordered her to look at the object he was holding, saying he had created it specially for her. She obeyed, and in that instant realized she was about to die. Terror took possession of her mind, but only for a moment. He penetrated her gently and made her climax one more time.

While her body was shaking with pleasure, something enormous and implacable began to make its slow way through her intestines. She attempted to wriggle free but managed only to arch her back. She wished she could die at once, but he wasn't letting her. He was good. He was the best she had ever met.

The cellphone in my shirt pocket vibrated. I continued to stare at the flickering green dot, while I decided what to do. I had too much alcohol in my body to think straight, so I answered it, just to get it off my mind. The deafening music forced me out onto the street.

It was Rudy Scanferla, who worked at my club: he even pretended he owned it. He said some guy had turned up who was in a hurry to talk to me. I replied I would be back the next day and clicked off. It was probably a client, but right then I was in no mood to listen to other people's troubles. I was having a better time than I'd had for years.

I was in the small Tuscan town of Pontedera, at Music Asylum, a store that sold CDs, vinyl and books, and belonged to a friend of mine, Guido Genovesi. We were celebrating, albeit rather belatedly, the birth of his daughter. The fact is I didn't pass that way very often. Four years earlier, I had walked into Music Asylum to buy a Canned Heat record and had found Guido there chatting and sipping aperitifs with a friend of his, Giacomo Minuti. We had taken a good look at one another and that was it: we were friends. After the shop closed we had gone on drinking and chatting in one bar after another, and when the very last landlord had shown us the door, we had climbed into

Giacomo's car and driven to the Piaggio village to watch the sun rise. It was a tight little district, built for the workers and employees of the famous scooter manufacturer which, for better or worse, had transformed the lives of just about everyone in the area. Giacomo had grown up there and reckoned that if you wanted to understand anything about Pontedera, here was the place to start. He was right.

I dropped in on Guido and Giacomo whenever I was within striking distance. Apart from running Music Asylum, Guido liked to write short stories. Giacomo, on the other hand, had a desk-job at the council offices in Vicopisano. One afternoon he had taken me on a tour of the town's castle and ancient jails. Prisoners there ground down the terracotta tiles of their cell floors, mixed the powder with water and used the resulting reddish paste to write and draw on the walls. I had been struck by the sketch of a steamship that an anarchist from Carrara, one Sirio Belletti, had made, during Fascism. It had made me long to run far away.

Giacomo didn't know I had been in prison. He and Guido had never asked me anything about my past, nor about how I made a living. I would have been forced to spin them some yarn about my present circumstances, but I would have told them the truth about my past; that I had spent seven years in prison, accused of terrorist offences. I wouldn't have wasted time explaining I was innocent. A pointless detail in the overall scheme of things. The night I blew my youth away, all I had done was let a guy I didn't know sleep at my flat. Then the cops had turned up, hooded and armed to the teeth. I had never seen the guy again – he was still in prison with a couple of life sentences to serve. I could have beaten the rap, but the judge insisted I recognize some persons I had never seen in my life before and who had done me no harm.

4

I was an ex-student and former blues singer, and prison had been hard on me. It had dried up my voice and fed a certain obsession with the truth. The kind that the blindfolded goddess of Justice never gets to see. On my release, I had exploited my reputation as someone who could keep his mouth shut and had used the experience I had gained in prison acting as a peacemaker between the various factions of the criminal underworld to carve myself out a profession as an unlicensed detective. It had turned out to be a smart move. Lawyers who needed an entrée into the criminal underworld to get their clients out of trouble were more than happy to come to me for help. My services didn't come cheap, but I almost always managed to stick my nose in the kind of places that investigating magistrates, cops and even ex-cop private investigators couldn't even think of approaching.

Business was brisk. I had bought myself a club just outside Padova. It was open only at night, was a good place to drink and the music was first-rate. Customers referred to it affectionately as La Cuccia, the dog basket. I had bought it because I needed a place where I could receive clients – a table kept permanently reserved in a strategic position from which I could keep an eye on the door, the bar and the stage. On account of my past, I had had to register La Cuccia in the name of Rudy Scanferla, my barman. He had been happy to accept the arrangement, enjoyed boasting about his club to the ladies, and the wages I paid him weren't bad either.

For my investigative work, I had two associates: Beniamino Rossini and Max the Memory. Rossini was a gangster of the old school. His father was from Milan but his mother was a legendary smuggler from the Basque country and it was her footsteps he had first chosen to follow, only later switching to holding up security vans. After a long interval spent in Italy's prisons, he had returned to cross-border trafficking, specializing in the Dalmatian coast, which he reached by high-speed motorboat. Lately he had been involved in recovering moneys hidden in the most improbable places, on behalf of prisoners unlikely to be released until well after the introduction of the euro, which was scheduled for 1 January 2002. Beniamino would go and pick up the proceeds from robberies and a variety of other illegal activities – on the strict understanding that neither narcotics nor child pornography had been involved – and would then pass the cash on to the right people to put it back into circulation, so that it could be converted into the new currency. Rossini hung on to twenty per cent of the sums recovered and naturally didn't have to issue receipts. His name, in any case, was as good as any guarantee.

He was rich enough not to need to take any part in my investigations, but the fact is that when we were in prison together I saved his life, and ever since he had made quite sure no harm ever came my way. Besides, he relished any kind of adventure. It made him feel alive. He had been married, but while he was residing at the state's pleasure his wife had betrayed him with his lawyer, abandoning him without a lira. He had taken no revenge and, frankly, I had never understood why.

On his left wrist, Rossini wore a collection of gold bracelets: one for every man he had killed. When it came to violence he was a true professional, using it to administer justice in accordance with the dictates of a gangland code now quite forgotten by the younger generation. Even though he was over sixty, he remained a redoubtable, implacable enemy. Tall, slim, still muscular, elegant, with dyed but thinning hair and a Xavier Cugat moustache,

Beniamino loved nightclubs and the women who frequented them. For the last few years, he had been seeing Sylvie, a French-Algerian bellydancer. It was a relationship typical of the nightclub world – lived from day to day, without any plans for the long term.

My other associate, Max the Memory, had gained his nickname on account of his passion for filing away all kinds of useful information. He had been accused of murder and of membership of an armed gang and had been on the wanted list for years, though in fact he had never left Padova. I had got to know him during one of my investigations, when I had needed information on some major operators who wanted me dead. At that time, Max was using his woman, Marielita, a South-American street artist, to do his spying in the city so he could keep his files updated. One day she was murdered by killers working for the locally based Brenta Mafia, and I was the one who held her in my arms as blood gushed from her belly and mouth. Max had never recovered from that loss and I, for my part, had never got over my sense of guilt, because Marielita and I had once spent a night together. It should never have happened.

Anyway, Max couldn't lie low for ever. They were bound to catch up with him sooner or later; they always did. Rossini and I managed to set up a trade with an anti-Mafia judge. It was the classic approach to justice: first you negotiate and then, when you've struck a deal, you go through all the rigmarole of the trial. In the end, the judge saw it was in his interest to help Max obtain a pardon after a relatively brief stay in jail.

When Max walked out of the gates of Rome's Rebibbia prison, I was there to give him a big hug and invite him to come and live at my place, in an empty flat over the club. He had accepted and from that day on we had been associates. His years in hiding and the loss of Marielita had left their mark. He spent a lot of time shut up in his study in front of his computer, smoking, drinking beer and grappa, and listening to good music. Prison had also bequeathed him a particular way of cooking. It was a solitary ritual, consisting of slow, measured motions that somehow enabled him to exorcise time and lick his wounds. Having filled the holes in his existence with food, tobacco and alcohol, he was overweight and his fingers were yellow with nicotine. I affectionately called him Fat Max, but never to his face. Max was touchy.

At the end of an investigation that had brought us into head-on conflict with a gang of Colombians, Max had decided to return to political activism. He wasn't content any more just to solve cases. Old Rossini and I had tried to talk him out of it because if he got into any trouble in the five years immediately following his release, his pardon could be revoked. The way things stood, a conviction for fly-posting could get him another fifteen years. He swore he'd be careful.

He had joined the so-called movement of movements, becoming what Italian newspapers refer to as a 'No Global'. He got involved in the fair-trade business, working for a Venice-based consortium of non-profit organizations that imported goods and produce from Africa, Latin America and Asia. There was nothing dangerous or illegal in this, but he had to take care not to lower his guard. The political climate in Italy had changed and anybody who thought that another world was possible was increasingly viewed as an enemy of Western democracy and civilization.

Whatever my misgivings, as a friend I had to feel happy for him. His smile was less sad now and he had recovered his interest in women. I had invited him to come with me to Pontedera but he had had some meeting to go to. He'd asked me to make a detour and drop in at his favourite pasticceria near Florence, to buy him a supply of good-quality chocolate. I would do that the following day, before returning to Padova and meeting the new client – assuming, that is, he would have the patience to wait for me.

Guido clapped me on the shoulder. 'Time for supper,' he said.

I smiled. I knew what my Tuscan friends meant by supper. We wouldn't be getting up from the table till at least two in the morning.

The client turned out to be a man in his fifties, tall, dark-haired and well-dressed. He got up to shake my hand. 'My name's Mariano Giraldi. Thanks for meeting me,' he said.

'What are you drinking?'

'Cognac, but I'm fine with this one.'

I motioned to Rudy to bring me a Calvados and lit a cigarette. While we waited, I took a closer look at Giraldi. He was nervous, clearly hadn't been sleeping and just couldn't wait to tell me his troubles. He adjusted the collar of his green Lacoste shirt and used his right thumb and index finger to stroke his salt-and-pepper moustache. His forehead and the hair at his temples were moist with sweat, despite the air-conditioning. He didn't look like a lawyer. Or a crook, for that matter. I hoped he was being cheated on by his wife: an easy and lucrative case.

'I'm listening,' I said abruptly.

'It's a complex business.'

'They always are. Take a nice, deep breath and tell me why you waited so patiently for my return.'

He stared at me, not appreciating my manners. For all I cared, he could lift his arse straight out of that chair and go right back to wherever he came from. But it was clear he had no intention of doing that.

'Listen, I hardly know where to start and you're not helping.'

My glass of Calvados arrived at last and I stuck my nose into the balloon-glass to savour its bouquet. 'Who told you to come to me?'

'Avvocato Bonotto.'

'An excellent reference.'

'He said you'd be able to help me.'

'Depends.'

'Someone's disappeared – a woman.'

'Wife, daughter, lover . . . Come on, don't make me beg.'

Again Giraldi stroked his moustache. 'Helena Heintze, my wife,' he said softly.

'When?'

'The sixth of June, about twenty days ago.'

'Took off with her lover?'

Giraldi shook his head and his eyes filled with tears. 'She's been kidnapped.'

I rummaged in my memory but couldn't recall any recent cases of kidnapping. As a crime, it was threatened with extinction. You needed a pretty big gang and, in the end, there was always somebody who squealed. Then, when it came to sentencing, judges handed down years and years. 'It's a police matter, so why have you come to me?'

'The police don't know she's been kidnapped. I just reported her disappearance, that's all. I said she left the house and didn't come back. It was even on television.'

'Why didn't you report it?'

'I couldn't.'

'You couldn't?'

'Helena was kidnapped in rather particular circumstances.'

'How particular?'

He cleared his throat. 'My wife is an S and M model,' he said, without taking a breath, no longer able to meet my gaze.

'Please go on.'

'I had gone with her to Turin, to a hotel near the airport where she had arranged to meet a client, but as soon as we walked into the room I felt this huge shock and fainted. When I came round, Helena had vanished, and I found this on the bed.'

He stuck his hand into an expensive-looking leather folder and passed me a strange object, some sort of white flower. Taking a better look, I realized it was made out of fine rope, soft and shiny as silk. An interminable series of minuscule knots fashioned to resemble a rose. I put it down on the table.

'What is it? The kidnapper's signature?'

'I don't know. There was nothing else in the room; even Helena's bag had gone. It was as if she'd never been there.'

'I'm afraid I don't understand you, Signor Giraldi. Why didn't you point the investigators in the right direction?'

Giraldi pulled a face and shook his head. 'Would you tell the police you had sadomasochistic fantasies and that your wife had been kidnapped by a client contacted on the internet?'

'Personally, I wouldn't go to the cops under any circumstances. But unlike you, I don't have a clean record and, even more to the point, I don't have a kidnapped wife.'

'Try to understand. Society views us as perverts and sadomasochism is an unmentionable sin. There is no community more clandestine than ours.'

'Paedophiles, maybe.'

'But we've got nothing whatever to do with that scum; we are all consenting adults.'

'Sure, including the guy who took off with your wife.'

Giraldi sighed. 'The world is full of psychopaths.'

'That's true enough. But a scene where people get tied up and whipped is bound to attract some evil weirdos – people who kidnap, torture their victims long and slow, and then kill them. Which may be precisely what has happened to your wife.'

Giraldi burst into tears. 'Help me, I'm begging you! I don't know what to do.'

'Stop snivelling, man, you're attracting attention,' I snapped, signalling to Rudy to bring my guest a drink. 'Knock it straight back; it'll do you good.'

Giraldi drained the glass of cognac and heaved a deep sigh. 'I'm a coward, I know, but I just didn't have the guts to tell the truth.'

'And the cops believed your story?'

'Yes, they did. They think we had a row and that she went back home to Germany.'

'And how did they come to that conclusion?'

'They wouldn't stop bombarding me with questions, so when one of them asked me if we'd had a falling-out, I replied that we had.'

'And had you really fallen out?'

'No.'

'Did you meet on the S and M scene?'

'No, we didn't. I'm a sales rep for a fabrics company. I started seeing Helena when she was trying, unsuccessfully, to launch a career as a fashion model, and I soon realized what her sexual preferences were. I was already familiar with the scene so I talked her into working as an S and M model.'

'Explain. I know nothing at all about the scene.'

'She posed as a slave for photographs.'

'Tied up and stuff like that?'

He didn't reply, but pulled out a photograph from his leather folder. Helena was a real beauty. Her long hair was gathered up in a perfect chignon and her face was in a slight shadow while her breasts were lit to perfection. A clothes peg was clamped to each nipple. Her hands and feet were bound by strips of leather to a wooden structure that vaguely resembled a St Andrew's cross.

'Right. I've got it. She's an S and M hooker.'

'No, you're wrong,' Giraldi said urgently, struggling to suppress his anger. 'Helena never had sex with her clients. Only photos.'

I pointed to the photograph with my index finger. 'But those pegs must hurt like hell.'

'She enjoys it.'

I took a closer look and saw he was right. The woman's expression showed neither pain nor disgust. 'So it's a genuine vocation.'

'Please don't be unpleasant, I beg you.'

'I'll do my best. How did clients get in touch with her?'

'On the internet. Helena places regular ads at specialist websites.'

'And where did they meet?'

'Usually in hotels or in rented photographic studios.'

'And you went along with her. Were you present at the sessions?'

'Yes, to make sure clients didn't get violent while she was tied up.'

'So you're a voyeur as well as a pimp?'

He clenched his fists. 'Can you understand why I didn't tell the police the truth?'

'I asked you a question.'

'Yes, I like watching. Happy now?'

'And did Helena like you to watch?'

'It was a kind of game of ours.'

'A game financed by Helena's clients.'

'I make good money in my work. The proceeds of the photo sessions all went to Helena.'

'How much did she make per . . . session?'

'It varied, but a minimum of two million lire, three or four times a month.'

'And she was kidnapped in Turin?'

'That's right. But we live in Varese. Obviously we never met clients there, to avoid being recognized.'

'Obviously. And did you often go to that particular hotel?'

'No, it was the first time. The rule is never the same place twice.'

'Who chose the venues? You or the clients?'

'The clients. We didn't want to leave any evidence we'd been there.'

'So the kidnapper must have had to present some ID to rent the room.'

'I guess so, yes.'

'Didn't you ask for any information at the reception desk?'

'No, I just fled in a panic.'

'And nobody saw you enter or leave the hotel?'

'No. It was nighttime. We slipped in through an emergency exit that the client had left open for us.'

Giraldi's story was full of holes. 'I don't believe a word you're saying.'

'You don't know the scene. We're constantly afraid of discovery ... ' he tried to explain.

'Okay, that I can understand. But even so, the way you behaved just isn't credible. You get knocked unconscious, your wife is kidnapped by some sadist, and you don't go to the police for help?'

'I've come to you for help.'

'After twenty days have elapsed.'

Giraldi didn't reply. He covered his face with his hands and started snivelling again. 'I didn't know what to do. I was terrorized. Then I had the idea of turning to a lawyer.'

'What do you think happened to your wife?'

'I don't know. I only hope she's still alive ... perhaps they just want to hold her at their disposal.'

I got Rudi to bring me another glass of Calvados. Then I picked up the photograph of Helena and tried to imagine what kind of trouble she'd got herself into. I couldn't think of anything other than murder. At the hands of a sadist. 'It's no easy matter kidnapping someone and then keeping her prisoner for a long time,' I said, thinking aloud.

'That's where you're mistaken. On the S and M scene, lots of people have their own dungeons, secret rooms specially equipped for sessions. I sense that Helena is still alive.'

'Then go to the police. When it suits them, cops can investigate quickly.'

'You still don't understand. I can't. Besides, the lawyer told me that now I might be a suspect myself.'

'Bonotto is right about that, but sometimes you have to run risks. It strikes me you're more concerned about your reputation than finding your wife.'

'That's not true.'

'Do you love her?' I asked point-blank.

'You can't possibly imagine how much.'

'I find that hard to believe. Is there anything else I should know?'

'I can't think of anything. So, will you accept the case?'

'I don't know. I'll have to talk it over with my associates. Come back tomorrow evening.'

Giraldi got up. I motioned to him to wait while I wrote a number on a paper napkin. 'Plus expenses, obviously. Is it within your means?'

'Certainly.'

He held out his hand. I pretended I hadn't noticed and asked Rudy to bring me a third Calvados. Giraldi walked towards the door, leaving on my table the rope rose and the photograph of his wife.

'She'll be long dead by now. We'd just be wasting time,' Old Rossini said, observing the strange rope flower.

Max poured himself a grappa. 'The story her husband fed you is really pretty incredible. If someone kidnaps the woman you love from right under your nose, you do whatever it takes to get her back and you certainly don't start thinking about the consequences for your reputation.'

I lit a cigarette. I had foreseen my associates' resistance and, deep down, I was none too sure about taking the case either. 'Giraldi is willing to pay well and it would be a police-free investigation. As I understand it, sadomasochists go to a lot of trouble to keep the cops away from their scene.'

Max snorted. 'That's just the problem. Giraldi has got our backs to the wall.'

'What do you mean?' I asked.

'There's a woman in the hands of some maniac, so we can hardly pretend nothing's wrong. We're going to have to try and find her,' Max replied.

Beniamino got up from the armchair. 'Yeah? Why? The real bastard here is her husband, who hasn't the courage to face up to his responsibilities. It's his problem. Fuck him.'

Max shook his head. 'Well, I don't feel I can just abandon

that woman to her fate. I don't want stuff like this on my conscience,' he said, showing Rossini the photograph of Helena.

'Max is right,' I said.

Rossini threw his arms out wide. 'But what's the point of going looking for a corpse? Besides, we don't know the scene. We can't even be sure we'll manage to find out anything.'

'We could give ourselves a deadline. Say two months?' I suggested.

'No, a month's enough,' Max said.

'So you've really got your minds made up,' the old gangster snarled. 'And when we discover who kidnapped and probably killed her, what do we do? Call the police, tell her husband, or . . .'

'Calm down,' I said. 'That's an issue we can tackle when the time comes.'

'You don't understand. I don't want to go chasing after maniacs.'

'Neither do I,' Fat Max retorted. 'But, like it or not, we're already involved.'

When Giraldi walked into the club, we were sitting at my table, drinking and smoking in silence. Old Rossini was in a foul mood, convinced he was jeopardizing his reputation as a self-respecting gangster by getting mixed up in this case. Giraldi nodded a greeting and I motioned him to take a seat. His face looked even more tired and strained than it had the previous day.

'These are my associates. We have some questions for you.'

'So are you taking the case?'

'We're thinking about it,' I replied.

'Tell us what happened at the hotel. We want to hear it from you,' Max told him.

This time Giraldi didn't need any begging, but he added nothing of interest to what he had already told me.

Beniamino finished his vodka and clicked his tongue to get the man's attention. 'So far you've described your wife's kidnapping as if only one person were involved – the so-called client...'

'Sure, Helena had an appointment with a client.'

'But there's absolutely no way that someone working on their own could have put you out of action and then carried off a woman from a hotel bedroom.'

'He probably knocked out Helena as well.'

'I don't doubt that. But he couldn't just have heaved her onto his shoulders and dumped her in his car boot all by himself. It just isn't believable.'

'So?'

'So your wife was kidnapped by more than one person,' Max interjected. 'And just maybe sadomasochism has fuck-all to do with it and you haven't told us the whole story.'

Rossini decided to add insult to injury. 'Right. Maybe you bumped her off yourself, the cops are getting suspicious and now you want to cover your arse with this kidnapping story.'

Giraldi turned white and broke out in a sweat. 'I told you the truth, I swear it. Help me find Helena.'

'Just explain to me why you think she's still alive,' Rossini goaded him.

Giraldi broke down and wept. The club was full and even though my table was out of the way a couple of people turned and looked in our direction. Giraldi seemed sincere enough but his story still stank. Rossini forced him to finish his cognac. Giraldi blew his nose and begged our forgiveness, then got up to go to the toilet.

'Well?' I asked my associates.

'The man's lying,' Beniamino declared.

'Yeah, he's lying about something all right. But I can't understand why. And I reckon he's telling the truth about the kidnapping,' Max said.

'So . . . do we accept the case?' I asked, looking at Rossini.

'We'd just be wasting time.'

'But not money. Anyway, don't worry about it, Beniamino. If you don't feel up to it, Max and I will take it on: just the two of us.'

He gave me a filthy look. 'You're playing the same trick as Giraldi, boxing me in.'

I smiled. 'Yeah, it's a mean trick. You know perfectly well that without you around Max and I would end up in a shitload of trouble.'

'I know, I know, and you're using it.'

Max chuckled. 'This way at least you can justify getting involved in the investigation.'

Rossini snorted. 'All right then. In any case, we won't find a damn thing.'

'Giraldi's on his way back over,' I warned.

'Well? What have you decided?' Giraldi asked.

'We'll take the case,' I said. 'But in a month's time if we still have no leads, we'll drop it.'

'All right,' Giraldi whispered, relieved. He put his hand in his pocket and pulled out an envelope. 'Here's the money.'

'Pass it to me under the table,' I told him. I ripped open the seal and took a look. Crisp five-hundred-thousand-lire notes.

Max handed Giraldi a notepad and pen. 'Jot down the names of the websites, the nickname Helena used in her adverts, your address, the address of the hotel ... and anything else that might be of use to us. Above all, the email address of the client who contacted your wife.'

'I don't have it.'

'What?'

'I don't know the password my wife used to access her emails. She took personal charge of all the contacts.'

'Better and better,' I grumbled.

As Giraldi began to write, Beniamino seized hold of his hand. 'If I find out you've told us bullshit I'll make you suffer, and if you tell the police about us I'll kill you.' Then he got up. 'I'll see you guys tomorrow.'

'That was valuable advice,' I said, 'and free of charge. If I were you, I'd keep it in mind.'

'There's no need to use these methods with me,' Giraldi hissed.

'Keep writing, Signor Giraldi. Keep writing and make quite sure you leave nothing out,' Max said placidly.

'What do you think, Max?' I asked, as we watched Giraldi head for the door.

'This rope flower gives me the creeps,' he replied, turning it over in his fingers.

'In what way?'

'It's perfect. Whoever made it is precise, imaginative and incredibly dextrous. Have you any idea how much pain a guy like that can inflict?'

'Enough to hope that death comes quickly.'

'Exactly. And he wanted Helena's husband to know it too.'

Early the next morning, Max and I weaved our way through the market stalls in Turin's Piazza delle Erbe and then entered the narrow streets of the ancient ghetto. We were heading for the rope shop belonging to Bianchin, an authority on everything to do with ropes and knots. We had got to know him while drinking in city-centre osterie. Whenever he could, he got one of his children to look after the store for him, took off his apron and repaired to the bars that ringed the square. We found him in his shop, intent on serving a lady customer, half a Toscano cigar, as always, hanging extinguished from the corner of his mouth.

'What can I do for you?' he enquired of us in the local dialect.

I took the rope flower from my pocket and placed it on the counter. The old shopkeeper donned a pair of glasses and observed it closely. Then, using his scissors, he cut through a single knot that formed the base of a petal and examined the rope's cross-section.

'Rich people's stuff,' he exclaimed, bemused. 'This cordage is hand-made. To order, no doubt, and not in Italy. Possibly in the Far East. The core is Dacron, the first sheath is Lilion and the second sheath, the outer one, is silk.'

'What else can you tell us?'

He resettled his spectacles on his nose. 'It's fine but highly resistant. The silk has a purely aesthetic function. It feels softer and more pleasing in one's grasp. Usually, this type of cordage is used in winches or snap-hooks because it runs well. It has the drawback that certain knots come undone more easily but whoever created this flower took great care to use the right knots: the Spanish hitch, the Fisherman's loop and, for the petals, a variation of the Turk's Head.'

'Do you know who could have made it?' Fat Max enquired.

'Someone with a lot of time to lose,' Bianchin replied curtly.

The old man had worked up a thirst so he invited us to go with him to a nearby osteria.

I looked round. 'You're on your own here, aren't you? Who's going to look after the shop?'

'Nobody, but I don't care. My children have decided to sell up so, after more than forty years here, this place is going to get turned into a shoe shop.'

As he drank his glass of Merlot, he recounted anecdotes from the old days, about Turin and its shops. When he'd finished talking he said goodbye with a bitter grimace. Just another old man shoved to one side.

'Bianchin's right; this city isn't what it was,' I remarked, glancing at the window of a smart boutique. Until a few years earlier, it had been a trattoria that fed generations of students.

'This city's dead,' Fat Max sighed. 'Throttled by money and shady deals.'

San Maurizio Canavese was only a few kilometres from Turin airport. We had arrived in the early afternoon and identified the hotel where Helena had been kidnapped. It was small, anonymous but comfortable-looking, the classic hotel for people passing through, strategically located close to a bypass. Just the place for sales reps, passing trade and people who didn't want to be noticed. The fire stairs led down to a car park at the back, surrounded by fields and far from any peeping eyes. The perfect place for slipping away with a kidnapped woman.

We decided to hand the night-porter some cash in exchange for the information that interested us and, since we had no better way of killing the intervening time and escaping from the heat of the afternoon, we took ourselves off to a good restaurant. Max had reserved a table for three at La Credenza, after checking that smoking was permitted. Nowadays, we always had to ask. Max had read glowing reviews of the place in a number of restaurant guides and couldn't wait to taste for himself the cooking of Giovanni Grasso, the chef and proprietor.

The premises were elegant and quiet, the diners chatting in low voices, focusing on pleasuring their palates. As always, faced with the menu I struggled to make up my mind and in the end followed the chef's recommendations. Max and Beniamino ate with relish, starting with antipasti. I made do with a fillet of beef in a raisin, saffron and lemon sauce, served on a bed of chick-pea purée. I hadn't touched a drop of alcohol all day and was thirsty. Nowadays I confined my drinking to the evenings, but I still had too much. At least that was what Virna thought. Before agreeing to get back together with me, she had insisted on a sharp reduction in my blood-Calvados level. After the cheese course, my associates ordered desserts and then, to round things off, coffees and liqueurs. Determined to restrict myself to just one glass, I went outside to make a phone call.

'It's me.'

'Ciao, Marco,' Virna said. 'Where are you?'

'Away. On a job.'

'When'll you be back?'

'Maybe tomorrow.'

'Shame. I'd hoped to see you before I left.'

'Left?'

'Yes. I'm going down to Gallipoli to stay with a friend of mine, Patrizia.'

'You didn't say.'

'I wasn't sure I was due any holidays. They make things so damn complicated at this club.'

'How long are you going to be away?'

'A month. I'm taking all the holidays I'm owed.'

'I'll miss you.'

'To be perfectly honest, I wanted to spend some time away from you.'

'And I thought we were growing closer.'

'That's exactly why. I want to think it over carefully.'

'I understand.'

'No, Marco, you don't understand. I love you but I'm not sure that's a good enough reason to stay with you.'

'That's a line I've heard before.'

'You've got so many problems, and you're always looking for more.'

'Have a nice holiday, Virna,' I said, clicking off.

I went back into the restaurant, where Max and Beniamino were chatting away merrily. 'Another Calvados,' I told the waiter.

'You look like someone who's just quarrelled with a woman,' Rossini commented.

'Virna's off on holiday to think about our relationship.'

'But hadn't you two got back together?' Max asked.

'That's what I thought, too.'

'As usual,' Beniamino broke in, 'you haven't understood a goddamn thing. A couple of fucks doesn't mean a relationship's back on track. The problems that led to you breaking up in the first place didn't just vanish while you weren't seeing each other. And they're not going to go away in the future, either.'

'Well, thanks for your encouragement.'

'Virna is a woman with very clear ideas about life, and she doesn't like the way you lead yours. What she wants is for you to ditch your investigations and devote yourself to the club full-time.'

'That's just not possible.'

'In that case, I can't see how you can have any future together.'

'Well, I can. I'm convinced we can find some way to make us both happy.'

'Bullshit,' Max said. 'Delude yourself as much as you like, but Virna's not a little girl any more. If you don't give her what she wants she'll leave you for good.'

'But what about Beniamino? He's been with Sylvie for years and everything's just sweet.'

'Sylvie's a nightclub dancer. She takes each day as it comes, just like we do,' Rossini pointed out.

I looked at my two associates. 'What's got into you two this evening, anyway? Just happen to be in the mood for handing out two-a-penny words of wisdom?'

'Not at all. It's just that whenever you get lovelorn you become a total pain in the arse and given that we've got our work cut out with this S and M business . . .'

'Okay, I've got the message. I promise you won't hear another word out of me about Virna.'

They both burst out laughing. Max looked at his watch. 'Instead of talking crap, pay the bill. It's time we went and had a word with the night-porter.'

'We'd like some information,' I said with a friendly smile. The night-porter, a bright-looking guy with fair hair, looked for a moment at the two banknotes, folded lengthwise, that I was holding tightly between my index and middle fingers.

'I'd like to be of assistance to you, providing it's nothing illegal.'

'All we want to know is who rented room 208 on the

evening of the sixth of June,' I said, placing the money on the reception desk. 'A simple glance at the register.'

He squirrelled the notes away in his jacket pocket, then opened the register and flicked rapidly through its pages. 'Here we are. The guest presented a driver's licence registered in the name of Mario Lo Bianco, who was born and resides in Monza . . . we even have a photocopy of the licence.'

Max jotted it all down while the night-porter made a fresh photocopy. 'To your knowledge, did anything happen that night?' I asked.

'Nothing. I was on duty and nobody brought anything to my attention.'

'And how did the guest pay?' Beniamino asked.

'I'd have to check the bills.'

'We'd really appreciate it.'

He vanished behind a door and returned after a couple of minutes. 'Cash in advance,' he said.

We could have guessed.

'The room's free,' Max said, pointing at the key-rack. There was a key attached to a number 208 tag dangling from a hook. 'Could we take a look?'

'No, I can't do that.'

I placed a one-hundred-thousand-lire note on the desk. 'We'll only be a minute.'

'Okay, but make it quick,' he said, reaching for the key.

Room 208 was at the far end of the ground-floor corridor, right next to the emergency exit. The client must have left it ajar so Giraldi and Helena could slip in unobserved and he had no doubt used the same door again later to carry the woman out. Beniamino opened the door to the room without making the slightest sound. To get to the bed you had to walk past the bathroom where, according to Giraldi's account, the kidnapper had been lying in wait to knock him out. From the description he'd provided we'd come to the conclusion that the assailant had probably used a stun gun. Silent and effective. We reconstructed the scene, and realized at once that there was no way the supposed client could have attacked Giraldi without Helena seeing what was happening and screaming for help.

'There must have been at least two of them,' Rossini said. 'One in the bathroom who put Giraldi out of action and another guy probably lurking back here, just out of sight, who took care of the woman.'

'If that's the case,' Max reasoned, 'we can discard one possibility right from the start. It can't have been a serial killer. They hardly ever operate in pairs.'

'We've got the photocopy of the driver's licence,' I observed. 'Maybe he's our man.'

'It's a fake,' Rossini stated categorically.

'Probably is,' Max added. 'But we'll still have to check it out.'

'Then let's do it immediately,' I suggested.

We returned the room-key to the night-porter and went back to the car. My associates had refused to travel in my Skoda Felicia, which was slow and had no air-conditioning, so we had made the trip in Old Rossini's Chrysler PT Cruiser. With its black metallic body and tinted glass, it looked like it belonged to a 1940s Chicago mobster. When I'd pointed out to Beniamino that it was too out of the ordinary to pass unobserved, he'd just shrugged. Any attempt to make him see sense would have been a total waste of time. A gangster of his generation would never give up his flashy car.

I inserted an Albert King cassette in the car stereo.

Immediately, the intro to 'Cadillac Assembly Line' blared out. 'This one's for you, Beniamino,' I said.

Rossini guffawed as he swung the car onto the Turin bypass and floored the accelerator. Max switched on the interior light so he could examine the photocopy of the driver's licence. 'It's not that clear. But it's clear enough for us to establish whether Signor Lo Bianco is our man.'

Max handed me the photocopy and I found myself staring at the faded likeness of a man of roughly forty or – according to the information on the document – exactly forty-two years old. An unremarkable face framed by straight, parted hair, and a beard trimmed short.

'It would be too neat if this was him,' I said.

'I already told you. That licence is a fake and the fact it's a fake should make us think,' Rossini said.

'What about?'

'Your everyday sex maniac doesn't go to the trouble of using fake identity documents. He wouldn't even know where to get them from.'

Max lit a cigarette. 'We know there were at least two people in that hotel room and they have the right contacts with criminal counterfeiters. This kidnapping is starting to look like the work of a gang that has nothing whatever to do with sex.'

'Maybe Giraldi has some debts outstanding with loan sharks or drug dealers.'

'Maybe. But why make up the S and M story? He could have told a less complicated fib.'

'You're forgetting the photograph of Helena, trussed up like a salami and with pegs on her nipples. S and M has got to come into it somewhere.'

Old Rossini turned into a service area. 'Could be. The problem is, what the fuck are we going to do once we've established that Signor Lo Bianco wasn't involved in the kidnapping?'

'I've got an idea,' Max replied. 'Helena was contacted by her kidnappers on the internet. I figure that's where we should start.'

'What if they've covered their tracks?'

'Then we're fucked.'

We filled the tank, then drank a coffee in a bar packed with truckers, drowsy car-drivers, prostitutes working away from their home patch and other miscellaneous nighttime fauna. Even the girls behind the counter were tired. Their drawn faces clashed somehow with their colourful uniforms, and sweat-soaked locks of hair stuck out of their regulation little hats. They reminded me of Virna when she cleaned the floor after the last customers had left the club. I felt the urge to have a drink, but I wasn't going to waste time asking for Calvados. I'd never seen a bottle of the stuff on any shelf in the bars that dotted the autostrada network.

I went down to the basement, following the signs for the toilets. A South American woman in her early thirties was sitting on a plastic chair between the door to the Gents and the door to the Ladies. There was a little dish for small change on a stool beside her. As I brushed past her she stared at me just to remind me that although I was allowed to piss for free a tip would be gratefully received. She stank of disinfectant. Stuck in that hole day and night, she had absorbed its smell. On my way out, I left her a ten-thousand-lire note. I'd charge it to Giraldi – travel expenses.

'I've no change,' the woman said.

'That's okay. Forget it.'

'You must have had some good luck this evening.'

'Not exactly.'

'I'll never be in a position to leave anyone such a huge tip.'

'You never know,' I lied. 'Life can change.'

I found Max and Beniamino at the checkout, paying for sweets, cigarettes and a Tom Waits cassette. There was a number on it I liked: 'Fumblin' with the Blues', and back in the car, I asked Max to put it on full-blast.

We reached Monza at about two in the morning. We could hardly turn up at Signor Lo Bianco's house at that hour so we went to a hotel where Rossini was treated as one of the family. They gave us three rooms without even opening the register. From the night-porter's behaviour, I could tell there was nothing unusual about this. It was the perfect hideout for anyone who'd just robbed a bank and needed to lie low till the cops decided to lift the roadblocks. A generous backhander would obviate any awkward questions relating to documents.

I stretched out on the bed and turned on the TV, selecting a local channel. An aged starlet was shouting herself hoarse in an effort to get viewers to splash out on authentic, antique Persian carpets. I'd heard she had taken to working for a shopping channel to fund her cocaine habit. From time to time a merciless close-up would throw her rosy-red nostrils into stark relief. She understood fuck-all about carpets and was reading the names off a piece of paper concealed in the palm of her hand. I had once seen Rossini beat up a fence who had walked up to him in a restaurant to offer him carpets that until a few days earlier had belonged to a wealthy local industrialist. The guy had been over-insistent and failed to realize that, as far as my associate was concerned, he was dealing in the wrong line of merchandise. Beniamino had invited him to step outside so they could

32

discuss terms and punched him in the face with a right hook followed by a straight left. He had then told the fence that he didn't like being disturbed at dinner and that, having recently seen a report on TV about the working conditions of children employed in carpet manufacturing, he could stick his Herats and Germetshes.

'The smaller the hands, the smaller the weaving knots. Can you believe those bastards?' Beniamino had explained to me, returning to our table.

Recalling that phrase now brought to mind another sort of knot, the kind used in the rope flower Giraldi had found in the hotel room where Helena was kidnapped. Max was right; that object was enough to give you the creeps. It was the product of pathological skill. At first I had assumed that Giraldi's wife had been the victim of a lone sadist who had carried her off to a house of horrors and tortured her to death. But having seen the room where the couple had been attacked, that scenario no longer made sense. There had perhaps even been a third kidnapper waiting in a car in the car park ready to make a quick getaway. But if it wasn't some sex maniac, why had Helena been kidnapped?

I heard a knock at the door. It was Rossini, already dressed and shaved. 'You didn't even get undressed for bed,' he said, tut-tutting.

'I was thinking about Helena.'

'The late Helena, you ought to say.'

'Are you really that sure?'

'After all these years, I've learnt to trust my instinct.'

'But we don't yet have a motive for the kidnapping.'

'So what? When there's no money involved, whoever's kidnapped always comes to a bad end. Come on, wash your face. Max is already downstairs having breakfast.'

Mario Lo Bianco lived in a huge block of flats on the outskirts of Monza. It was eight a.m. when I rang the bell. A woman in a dressing-gown opened the door.

'Is your husband at home?'

'He left at six for the factory, like every other day.'

I showed her the photocopy of the driver's licence. 'Is this him?'

'No. That's not Mario.'

'Has he by any chance mislaid his licence?'

'No, he hasn't, I'm sure of it. Excuse me, but who are you?'

'The police, Signora. It's just a routine check,' I replied, walking away.

'Drew a blank,' I told my associates.

'What did I say?' Rossini said complacently.

'Let's go home,' Max suggested.

'What if we drove to Varese, dropped in on Giraldi and had a look around?'

'For the time being, let's stay away from that guy. If, as I think, he's told us a pack of lies, he's probably under police surveillance,' Beniamino said.

'Right,' Max said with a nod. 'Let's try the internet first.'

We arrived home at around eleven a.m. Rossini said goodbye and went off to see Sylvie. For a moment, I envied him. Not only because he had a woman, but also because I'd always liked Sylvie. On more than one occasion, when watching her perform her belly-dancing routine in night-clubs, I'd realized to my surprise that I fancied her. But I'd limited myself strictly to fleeting thoughts. The women of one's friends are off limits. Besides, I knew I wasn't her type.

I followed Max into his flat. He switched on the

computer and connected to the net, then tapped in the first of the website addresses that Giraldi had given him. When the home page came up, he ran down a list of dominators, dominatrixes, couples, male slaves, female slaves, transsexuals, fetishists and switchers, and then clicked on female slaves.

'Helena's ad is here.'

I moved nearer the screen. 'Model with a passion for live performance available to BDSM enthusiasts for photographic and video sessions. Excited and eager for new thrills and experiences and ready to submit, with my master present, to bondage and punishments administered by genuine and sophisticated experts. Can travel North-Central Italy.'

'Now what?' I asked.

'We take a look at the other websites.'

We soon found ourselves confronted with thousands of ads. Max began patiently to scroll through the webpages. I tired of it within minutes.

'Helena's ad only appears on two websites,' Max said after a while. 'At least we've narrowed down our field of research.'

'I don't follow. What is it you want to do?'

'If we want to find out what's really happening on this scene, we need to hack into inboxes.'

'Do you know how to?'

'No, I don't. But I know people who do.'

He picked up his cellphone and punched in a number. 'Ciao Arakno, it's Max. I need your help. No, I can't explain exactly what it is, but you'd better bring some decent kit with you. Yeah, tomorrow's great. See you there.'

'Who were you talking to?'

'A guy called Arakno. To him and his partner Ivaz,

computers hold no secrets. They'll help us to break into people's emails.'

'Can we trust them?'

'Sure. I've known them a while. But we'd better lay in a couple of cases of Ichnusa beer, otherwise they can be a bit work-shy.'

'I'll tell Rudy to have some delivered. Judging by their taste in beer, they're Sardinian, right?'

'Correct. They'll get a flight from Cagliari tomorrow. I'll pick them up at the airport.'

'So I suppose till then we've not got much to do.'

'That's right. I'm going to cook myself a decent lunch and then I'm off to the fair-trade association for a meeting. Do you want to stay and have a bite?'

'No thanks. I'm going to take a shower and then go have a chat with Avvocato Bonotto. I want to get hold of some more information on Giraldi.'

My flat was dark and cool. The high ceilings and thick walls, reminders that the building had once been a barn, kept out the worst of the summer heat. I took a bottle of fizzy mineral water from the fridge – never could stand the flat stuff – and poured two fingers of fifteen-year-old Roger Groult into a glass. Virna was away, so what the hell. I switched on the TV to watch the regional news. In Padova, a gay rights centre had been set on fire. Rival criminal gangs, all of North African origin, had clashed near the train station. A couple of gang members had ended up in A&E with stab wounds. In the Vicenza area, a police quick-response team had uncovered yet more sweat-shops employing Chinese labour in conditions of semi-slavery. Near Treviso, on the other hand, a gang of Albanians had attacked an isolated villa. I switched off the TV, picked up another remote and selected a Bob Dylan CD. 'Tombstone Blues' poured out of the speakers.

The shower made me long for a fuck, but another glass of Calvados made the longing subside. I got dressed, put the rope flower in my pocket and walked out into the street, plunging into torrid two p.m. heat. I found Renato Bonotto in a city-centre eatery that sold exorbitantly priced salads. As always, he was on his own, seated at his usual table, looking slim and elegant. He was a skilful lawyer: even investigating magistrates respected him for his fair-mindedness. I had first met him when a client of his had been framed as the offloader for a consignment of Colombian cocaine, and ever since then he'd made regular use of me as an investigator.

'Ciao, Marco,' he greeted me. 'Can I get you something?'

'Thanks. I think I'll have one of those little open sandwiches.'

'To what do I owe the visit?'

'You sent me a rather strange client.'

'Giraldi ... the sadomasochist?'

'That's the one.'

'I don't know the man personally; he was referred to me by a colleague in Varese.'

'So you've never actually met him?'

'No, I haven't. But I trust my colleague implicitly.'

'Look, what do you know about this guy?'

'Just what he told you, more or less.'

'And what do you think?'

'That he made a mistake not going immediately to the police, but now it's too late. They'd throw him straight in jail.'

'Did he give your colleague in Varese the same version you got?'

'Sure. I checked before I handed him your name.'

I ate my sandwich in silence while Bonotto conducted a conversation on his cellphone, then I shook his hand and left. My Skoda was parked full in the sun and my shirt stuck to my shoulders the moment I leaned back in the seat. Ten minutes later I was on the autostrada heading for Varese. My associates wouldn't have approved. Giraldi might be under police surveillance and the cops would be very interested indeed to discover he had a connection with three ex-cons. But I needed to see where Helena had lived to get a clearer picture of the woman we were looking for. That photograph of her in the S&M pose didn't tell me anything; it just made me feel uncomfortable. It wasn't so much the pegs crushing her nipples as the expression of pleasure on her face.

Mariano and Helena Giraldi had a house on a new development in the middle of the countryside. I drove past a couple of times looking for signs of surveillance, but couldn't see any. No suspicious-looking cars or vans parked in the street. Almost every house was protected by CCTV and large, dangerous-looking dogs. Giraldi's place seemed deserted, but there was a white Mercedes in the drive. I parked in a parallel street and approached on foot to a chorus of barking dogs. At the front gate, I pressed the buzzer on the video-entryphone. I didn't have to wait long. Giraldi came out and attached his Argentine dog, a huge beast with watery and decidedly unfriendly eyes, to a chain.

'Any news?' he asked, as he opened the gate.

'No.'

'Then what are you doing here?'

'Just visiting,' I snapped back. I couldn't stand the guy.

He showed me into a large, expensively but tastelessly furnished lounge.

I stared at him. He was in an even worse state than the last time I'd seen him. His face looked ravaged with stress. He hadn't had a shave for days, his eyes were bloodshot and ringed with deep, dark shadows.

His cellphone rang, and the house suddenly echoed to an electronic version of one of the previous summer's pop songs. Giraldi glanced absent-mindedly at the number on the display. 'What can I do for you?' he asked, switching off the phone.

'I want you to sit down while I take a look around.'

'Why?'

'The only thing I know about your wife is that photo of her in the two-million-lire-a-session slave pose. I want to know the rest.'

Mariano Giraldi flopped in an armchair. 'Do as you please,' he muttered, with a wave of his hand.

I went upstairs, opened a door at random, and walked into a bathroom in which every single object clearly belonged to a man. Helena's bathroom was opposite. I went in, opened her cupboard and rifled through the creams and perfumes. Strictly nothing but brand-name products. Helena treated her body kindly. There were two bedrooms, too. I rummaged through Helena's bedside cabinets and her wardrobe, which was full to bursting with dresses and only two pairs of trousers. The woman liked showing her legs. She had a well-assorted and sophisticated range of underwear. But there wasn't a single item that would make you think of sadomasochism. I supposed Giraldi had had a clear-out after the kidnapping.

I went back downstairs and inspected the kitchen, then went down to the basement. Part of it was used as a garage and contained an Alfa Romeo coupé – Helena's. The remainder consisted of a large room, completely empty. The walls had recently been repainted in some shade of beige. I took out my car keys and scratched at the paint. A layer of white emerged, then, below that, one of black. Looking closer at the ceiling and walls, I saw that a number of holes had recently been filled. I imagined a pitch-black room fitted with some wooden contraptions. Helena and Mariano's erotic play-room.

'I see you dismantled your dungeon in a bit of a hurry,' I said, sitting down on the sofa opposite Giraldi.

'I was afraid the police would come and search the house.'

I lit a cigarette. 'So what else did you get shot of?'

'A couple of objects and some items of clothing.'

'There aren't any contraceptives in the house. How come?'

'That's none of your business. Concentrate on finding my wife.'

'I asked you a question. If you don't answer it, I'll hang on to your money and you can go fuck yourself.'

'Our sexual relations were . . . incomplete,' he said, staring at the marble-tiled floor.

'Meaning?'

'Helena didn't want to be penetrated.'

'I get it. And that was okay with you, was it?'

'I respected her desires.'

'What I want to know is whether you were happy just to jerk off or if you felt the need to stick your dick in some other place.'

'No need to be offensive.'

'Fine. Was the question clear enough or do I have to reword it?'

'I understand what you want to know. Helena is bisexual.

We had a three-way relationship, involving another woman.'

'Within the S and M scene?'

'That's right. She was a slave.'

'So that's what the room in the basement was for,' I said, thinking aloud. 'And was it with this other woman that you had penetrative sex?'

'Yes.'

'And how long had this arrangement lasted?'

'Since before we got married. The other woman has been my slave for years.'

'Signor Giraldi, you really are full of surprises. How many more have you got in store for me?'

Giraldi continued to stare at the floor in silence. His face had become a stone mask. He realized how vulnerable and defenceless he had become. I could see now why he hadn't gone and told the police about the kidnapping. They'd have turned him inside out, trampled all over the way he lived and made a mockery of his right to fuck any damn way he felt fit.

'I don't give a shit about your sexual tastes. The way I see it, consenting adults are entitled to have fun any way they like. The thing is, your wife has been kidnapped and I need to know everything there is to know about her. Then, once we've fulfilled our side of the contract, my associates and I will forget the whole thing. Just like we always do.'

'What do you want to know?'

'I want to meet the other slave.'

'Why? She can't help you in any way.'

'I'll be the judge of that.'

'No way. This one's my decision. You're not meeting her.'

'Are you scared she might tell me something I'm not supposed to know?'

'It's just a waste of time. Anyway, as I'm paying you have to do what I say.'

I gave him a sidelong grin. 'That's not the way it works. Once we've accepted a case, we pursue our investigations in whatever way we deem fit and our clients just have to get used to it. So, right now, either you call this woman or I call my associate. You know, the nasty one.'

'Are you threatening me?'

'Sure am. For the sake of your wife.'

Giraldi reached for his phone. 'Use mine,' I said, handing him my cellphone. 'There may be a tap on yours.'

'Antonina, it's me. As soon as you get off work, come straight over to my place . . . I don't give a fuck about your husband; think up some excuse.' The authoritarian tone he'd assumed hardly seemed to belong to the same grief-stricken man I'd been speaking with a moment earlier.

I pointed this out to him, but he shrugged it off. It was just the way he was accustomed to talking to that woman, he explained. A simple matter of roles. I decided to play up mine and demanded he show me his photograph collection – I'd noticed a Polaroid camera in a drawer – and he got up and fetched a thick leather-bound photo album from the chimney. I advised him to think up a better hiding-place. The cops would have found it in a matter of minutes. I began to flick through the album: Helena tied and strung up in every imaginable position. Helena in a clinch with the other slave. Ropes, chains, leather masks, and the women's skin shiny with sweat. Giraldi didn't make a single appearance. There was even a poem signed by a certain Barbie Slave.

My head against Your bare belly
Your hands in my hair
Master . . .
Your games flutter over me, like butterflies over a meadow.
Your voice that slips hot inside me . . .
Making me a gift of sensations . . .
Master,
I love Your eyes, which bind me to You.
I love Your mouth, which marks my heart,
I love Your hands that touch my soul.
Master,
In Your castle Your slave
waits to fulfil Your desire . . .
As the moon is pierced
By the rays of the rising sun,
to remind the world of the regality
of its Master,
I await to be pierced by Your love,
to show to the whole world
the beauty of our love.

Total horseshit, I thought, handing the photograph album
back to its owner. In Italy everyone feels they're a poet.
Even when it comes to saying how sweet it is to have their
arses whipped.

'Satisfied?' Giraldi asked icily.

'Yes. I wanted to be sure no one else was involved. Given
that you still claim you know of no motive for the
kidnapping, I'm forced to lift your carpets and search for
dirt.'

'You don't believe me?'

'Less and less.'

The doorbell rang. A young woman's face, framed with a

bob of thick black hair, appeared on the video-entryphone. Giraldi let her in and the dog wagged its tail merrily: clearly a regular visitor. When she saw me, she blanched.

'This is one of the people helping me look for Helena,' Giraldi hurried to explain. 'He wants to ask you a few questions.'

'Why?' she asked, her voice quavering. 'I don't know anything.'

I observed her. She was short but fairly well-proportioned, with two skinny legs sticking out of a short, peach-coloured, low-necked dress. Her face was plain and there was a scar from an operation on her upper lip. She must have been in her early thirties. She was frightened, and to make her talk I decided to adopt the same tone Giraldi had used with her.

'Are you Barbie Slave?'

'Yes.'

'What's your real name?'

'Antonina Gattuso.'

'Are you married?'

'Yes.'

'Your husband's full name?'

'Silvio Cavedoni.'

'Any children?'

'A little girl.'

'You got a job?'

'I work in an office.'

'You have a relationship with Giraldi and his wife, is that correct?'

'No. We're only friends.'

'Bullshit. I've seen the photos. Do you want me to show them to your husband and work colleagues?'

44

The threat had no effect. She looked at Giraldi, who with a nod of his head commanded her to answer my question.

'Yes. We used to meet here.'

'Just the three of you?'

She didn't reply and again looked over at Giraldi. 'Answer!' I screamed.

'Occasionally Master Mariano orders me to have sex with other masters. As a punishment. When I behave badly . . .'

I turned to Giraldi. 'Go take a shower,' I barked.

'I'm telling you: this stuff has got nothing whatever to do with Helena's kidnapping.'

'Get out of here. I want to talk with this lady alone.'

Giraldi obeyed reluctantly. On his way out, he gave his slave a long, hard stare. It was a warning not to say too much.

'Sit in that armchair,' I ordered the woman, going to stand behind her. An old police trick. 'Why did you call him "Master"?'

'Because Mariano *is* my master. He has been training me to become a true slave.'

'For how long?'

'Seven years.'

'Are you a slow learner or what?'

'You have no idea . . . It can take an entire lifetime to attain perfection.'

'What are your feelings for Giraldi?'

'Devotion, love, and gratitude. I owe him everything. I was unhappy and unsatisfied until he chose me. Now I'm a complete woman.'

'Because he whips you and ties you up?'

'That's only one aspect. I need to feel humiliated and submissive.'

'Well, what about your husband?'

'He's never understood me. We were already engaged to be married when I met Master Mariano.'

'And he's never had any suspicions?'

'No.'

'You're telling me you've been on the S and M scene for eleven years and he knows nothing about it.'

'That's normal. Everyone involved in S and M leads a double life.'

'In other words, you're a wife, a mother, an office-worker, and then once a week you become a slave?'

'Yes.'

'And do you love your husband?'

'Sure.'

'So you love two men.'

She shook her head. 'They're different kinds of love. They complement one another.'

'And are you happy like this?'

'Yes, I am.'

'Then why are you frightened?'

'Because of what's happened to Helena,' she replied, after a brief hesitation.

'Are you afraid you'll be kidnapped too?'

'No. I'm afraid of the police. I'm scared they'll find out everything and it'll all become public knowledge. My whole life, and that of my family too, would be destroyed.'

'So you don't give a damn about Helena.'

'She's Master Mariano's wife.'

'But you made love with the woman.'

'That was part of the training.'

'You mean you didn't enjoy it?'

'If my Master enjoyed it then I enjoyed it too.'

'What do you know about the kidnapping?'

'Nothing. Only what Master has told me.'

I took the rope flower from my pocket, walked round to the front of the armchair and showed it her. 'Do you know what this is?'

'No, I don't.'

I pointed to the door. 'You can go, and if you're really worried about your reputation, stay away from Master Mariano until Helena's been found.'

She didn't need to be told twice. I sat down in the armchair, lit another cigarette and began to think. Antonina Gattuso hadn't been able to tell me anything useful about the kidnapping, but she had enabled me to understand a lot about the kind of relationships people on the S&M scene had with one another. Playing a role was not a performance they put on just to have some enjoyable sex. There was something deeper that drove people to construct perfectly organized double lives. It was vital that nobody outside the S&M scene should know a thing, not even their nearest and dearest. Discovery would destroy their lives totally. What Antonina had said might seem like the ravings of some pathetic half-wit. But it wasn't like that. Somehow, she had found in this relationship of absolute physical and psychological dependency on Master Mariano an equilibrium that made her life easier to live. She had even said she was happy.

If Helena really had been 'disappeared', finding her would not be easy. The danger of being unmasked and disgraced compelled anyone on the S&M scene to use rules and codes hard for any outsider to decipher. I couldn't help wondering if we were really up to the job. Out of the corner of my eye I noticed Giraldi standing in the middle of the room, watching me with a worried look on his face. I got up and left without saying goodbye.

That night La Cuccia was crowded; Maurizio Camardi and

his band were playing, and he greeted me with a nod of his saxophone. Max and Beniamino were sitting at my table eating chocolates and drinking Sicilian Ala Amarascato wine. Rudy brought me an Alligator iced to just the right temperature, while I talked about the visit I had paid Giraldi, told them what I had been thinking and how I was worried we might never understand such an inaccessible scene, let alone manage to investigate it.

'They have to communicate among themselves somehow,' Max pointed out. 'If we can just penetrate their information systems, we'll be able to read them like a book.'

'Assuming your Sardinian friends can break the passwords.'

'I don't have any doubts on that score. The problem is, we don't yet know what we're looking for.'

'One beautiful German blonde,' I said.

'What did this Antonina Gattuso look like?'

'Not much.'

'Do you reckon she told you the truth?'

I let my cocktail slip down slowly. 'I don't know. They're so used to lying that I kind of assume she didn't tell me the whole story. The same goes for Giraldi.' I reached for a chocolate.

Max's face puckered with disgust. 'It's wasted with that brew you're drinking. Have it with some wine; it brings out the taste of almonds.'

'Wine's not my drink. I prefer my "brew".'

'You're a hopeless barbarian,' Rossini chuckled. 'Any attempt to educate your palate is doomed.'

'Look who's talking. As I recall, we wolfed down precisely the same prison swill yet now it seems all that time you were really some kind of gourmet.'

'By the way,' Max said, 'I don't know about you two, but this whole S and M thing has got me thinking about prison.'

'I don't want to talk about it,' Beniamino snapped.

'Nor do I,' I said.

'But you *have* been thinking about it,' Max continued, undeterred. 'It's reminded me of a couple of prison officers who were sadistic, in the true sense of the term.'

'Stop it,' I hissed. 'Why do you want to ruin our evening? We all know there are some pretty sick people in prison, among both prisoners and screws.'

'Except that if it's a prisoner it's a problem you can solve, whereas if it's a screw, you just have to put up with unending gratuitous harassment.'

'Tell me something I don't know,' I retorted. 'Jails are the ideal place for every kind of frustrated nutter – people who only feel they're somebody if they've got a uniform on their back.'

'I wasn't talking about that. I was referring to the fact that some of the screws I got to know had a genuinely sadistic side to their character.'

'If you carry on with this crap, I'm going to get up and leave,' Rossini warned. 'You know damn well there are certain prison experiences you just don't talk about. It's shit that everyone has to deal with on his own.'

'Beniamino's right.'

'But the thing is, this shit, as you call it, never goes away. You know that. It gets stuck in your brain.'

'Precisely. And as there's no way you can forget it, there's absolutely no point keeping on dredging it up.'

'I don't agree.'

'Then go see a shrink.'

'I can only talk about prison with people who've been inside.'

'Then I really don't know how to help you.'

Maurizio came over and sat down at our table, which put an end to the argument. We got talking about music and musicians and the mood relaxed. Later, however, when I returned to the solitude of my flat, the memories Max had stirred resurfaced in my mind as from a brimming sewer. Max was right when he said there was something about the S&M scene that was reminiscent of prison, but I couldn't work out what it was; maybe the use of chains, coercion and physical violence. Or maybe it was the clear-cut division between roles, with the torturer on one side and the victim on the other, like screws and prisoners. It certainly put me on edge. I recalled a young Calabrian transvestite hooker I had got to know in the isolation wing of the San Giovanni in Monte prison in Bologna. He was there because his appearance was too feminine for him to be held in the main block. I was there because I was in transit, awaiting transferral to the main prison in Padova, and the governor in Bologna didn't want too many 'politicals' on the loose in his prison. The transvestite had been arrested for robbing a client. Every night a bunch of prison officers and prisoners went to his cell, made him dress up like a woman and put on make-up, then gagged him, tied him to the bars of his cell and took it in turns. I could hear everything but just sat smoking in the dark, wishing they'd hurry up and leave. In the mornings, during the exercise hour, I hadn't the guts to look him in the eye, and did everything I could to avoid him. Now, I could no longer remember his face, just his smothered screaming.

I got out of bed and went to the kitchen for a drink. If I'd gone on recalling stuff, other ghosts would have emerged and I couldn't let that happen, couldn't run the risk of plunging into my own personal abyss of pain and shame for the humiliations I'd suffered. I had never been the object of sexual abuse, but I knew full well that prison spawns every conceivable aberration.

I phoned Virna but her cellphone was switched off, so I pulled on my trousers and went and knocked on Max's door. He was still awake, and came to the door with a book in his hand.

'Thanks to you, I can't sleep,' I said as I walked in.

'Nightmares from a recent past?' he asked sarcastically.

'Fuck off, Max.'

'Do you want to talk about it?'

'No. What the hell are you playing at? Do you want to turn us into some kind of prison-survivors' self-help group?'

'Might be an idea.'

'Cut the crap and give me a drink.'

He pointed at the sideboard. 'Help yourself.'

'What are you reading?'

'*A Treatise on Sadomasochistic Perversion* by Franco De Masi.'

'And what does it say?'

'That sadomasochism is a dangerous perversion, involving the "sexualization of a destructive pleasure".'

'*No*, really?'

'The author says that sadomasochistic relationships produce a state similar to a drug-induced high so that the dose of violence tends to keep increasing.'

'What about those on the receiving end? Do they manage to endure it?'

'Yeah, it seems so. Pain prompts the nervous system to manufacture endorphins, which create a sense of wellbeing, sometimes even ecstasy.'

'And what do you think?'

51

'I still think that within limits people should be free to fuck whatever way they like.'

'What limits?'

'Well, those stipulated at the specialist S and M websites. What they rather pompously refer to as the "ethical and behavioural codes of sadomasochistic orthodoxy". In short: safe, healthy and consensual sex. What's more, there's a series of rules on how to negotiate play boundaries and some agreed safe words for calling time-out.'

'If they're that wary they've obviously encountered problems in the past.'

'Big problems, judging by the straightforward but effective safety regulations they've developed to avoid falling into the hands of the wrong people.'

'Like those who kidnapped Helena.'

'Precisely. These guys are like wolves prowling for their prey in a world of secrets and enforced silence. Giraldi's behaviour provides a striking illustration.'

'I get the feeling that Helena and Giraldi failed to follow safety procedures.'

'They totally ignored them and I'd really like to understand why. Going on what you discovered at their house, it's pretty clear that Giraldi and his wife had been actively involved in the S and M scene for years. But they walked into that hotel room with their eyes shut tight. The guidelines stipulate that the initial meeting must be arranged in a public place and in the presence of a friend who can act as a monitor, keeping an eye on the situation from a distance. What's more, the first time they have sex, it's forbidden to tie up the submissive partner – precisely in order to prevent anything untoward.'

'I just can't believe Giraldi and his wife let themselves be duped like a pair of absolute novices.'

'Nor can I, which is another reason for rejecting Giraldi's version of events.'

'Did you get any other insights from surfing the S and M websites?'

'Analysing the data, I noticed that women are a small minority, whether as slaves or as mistresses. The biggest group of S and M practitioners consists of men wanting to be subjugated, closely followed by men wanting to be masters. After that, there are fetishists and various other sub-categories. In all, there are tens of thousands of people on the circuit.'

'We can't check them all out.'

'Helena advertised as a slave. That's where we start our search.'

My cellphone woke me just before midday. It was Max the Memory. 'I'm on my way back with our guests,' he announced. I surreptitiously made myself a mug of instant coffee and added two fingers of Calvados. Max would be horrified if he found out and would cut me dead: as far as he was concerned, fair-traded coffee was the only option. It was good, true enough; indeed it was the best coffee you could get, but in the morning all I wanted was this instant brand, strong, plentiful and sugary, in one of those red mugs they give away with four packet tops. A proper coffee-maker, bubbling away on the gas-ring alongside a solitary cup, would have reminded me of prison. I cursed Max yet again. I had been doing my best to forget the seven years I had spent behind bars and now he demanded we sat round a table to rake over our nightmares.

I lit the first cigarette of the day and thought of Virna. I tried to call her again but she couldn't be reached. She had clearly decided not to speak to me while she reappraised our relationship. I carefully chose a CD to put me in a good mood – 'Moondance' by Van Morrison – then stepped under the shower. Max had given me an entire range of excellent and healthy natural toiletries and I'd never touched them. I used supermarket shampoo and body wash. I liked them garish, creamy and fragrant. The one I now smeared all over my chest and thighs smelled of citrus fruit, nice and summery, just like the ads promised.

The Sardinian hackers arrived. They were tall and thin and couldn't have been a day over twenty-five. Ivaz sported short, dark-brown hair, whereas Arakno's was red and shoulder-length. Both of them had tattoos on their arms, clearly done by the same talented artist. They certainly hadn't been done in prison. Tattoos were the height of fashion right now but you didn't often see such fine ones. Max and I were among the few ex-cons who didn't have any; neither of us liked the idea of having to look at the same drawing for an entire lifetime.

'They're a pair of kids,' I whispered to Max.

'So what? So were we once,' Max said. 'Anyway, don't worry, they come highly recommended.'

Ivaz and Arakno said hello, opened their metal cases and started pulling out laptops, modems and cables of every dimension.

'You've certainly brought enough kit with you,' I remarked in astonishment.

Arakno snickered. 'This is just the key that gets us into the serious hardware.'

'These laptops,' Ivaz added, 'will enable us to log on to our university intranet. A guy we work with will then connect them up to the internet so they can go to work for us. We'll tell them what they need to look for.'

While they were setting up their equipment, I went down to the club and got a case of Ichnusa beer from the fridge. They were really grateful and got straight down to work, cigarettes hanging from the corners of their mouths.

Fat Max connected to one of the two sites where Helena

had posted her ads. 'The first thing I want to do is get into this inbox: helena at . . .'

'Let's see what we can do,' Arakno said. 'I'm going to use the intranet to randomly generate some passwords, while Ivaz tries to sort through them using the prompts that the systems manager suggests when the user forgets their password.'

'You've lost me,' Max said.

'Any time you open an email account, you're asked to provide a question, the answer to which reminds you of your password. Sometimes it's really simple, like a husband's name or a date of birth.'

Max reached for a notebook, jotted down all the data we had on Helena and handed it to Ivaz.

'Why don't you put some music on?' Arakno asked. 'My ears are still buzzing from the plane engines.'

Max switched on the CD in the computer drive. It was a jazz track, but it reminded me of a well-known tune. 'I've heard another version of this somewhere.'

Max chuckled. 'It's Renato Sellani's trio playing a set of Ricky Gianco numbers. To be precise, this piece is called . . .'

'"Pugni Chiusi"' Ivaz said. He began to hold forth on the various different versions of 'Pugni Chiusi' but was soon interrupted by Arakno announcing that he'd managed to access Helena's inbox. Max and I approached the screen. Every message prior to the day of the kidnapping had been deleted and all subsequent messages were from old or new clients suggesting meetings. There was nothing there that could help us in our investigations.

I lit a cigarette. 'I don't reckon it was Helena who deleted those emails,' I said, thinking aloud.

'Nor do I,' Max said. 'It was either her husband or her kidnappers.'

'Giraldi said he didn't know what her password was,' I remarked. 'Besides, it's her kidnappers who had to avoid leaving any trace.'

'Is there no way of recovering them?' Max asked

Arakno took a sip of beer. 'No, there isn't. Every single message has been deleted, whether received or sent.'

'So what do we do now?' I asked, feeling disheartened.

'We just keep on poking our noses into the slaves' inboxes, hoping we get lucky.'

Max went off to fix some lunch while Arakno and Ivaz got back to work. It took them about twenty minutes to hack into the email account of a certain Anais '72 @ . . . , a 29-year-old from Novara, near Milan. She had posted her ad about ten days previously and so far she'd had replies from around seventy masters and mistresses. Several of them had left their cellphone numbers and at least half had attached photos of themselves in dominant poses, kitted out with the usual armoury of masks and whips. Sifting through the replies that Anais '72 had sent, it became apparent that she had selected three men from the Turin area and had now begun, with extreme caution, to exchange emails with them.

By the time Max returned from the kitchen, drying his hands on a dishcloth, I'd read through the inboxes of four different slaves. One of them had already started seeing a master, but was adhering strictly to the safety guidelines recommended at all S&M websites. The same masters' and mistresses' nicknames kept recurring and identical replies were frequently sent to different people. Sex slaves were evidently a rare commodity.

'We're going to have to come up with some other system,' Max grunted. 'This'll take us ages.'

'Yeah, you're right,' Ivaz said, stretching. 'But right now I'm hungry.'

Max had prepared linguine with a cream sauce containing prawns and aubergine, which Ivaz and Arakno ate with relish. Max and I were unable to concentrate on our food, too busy trying to think up some way of weeding through inboxes and saving time. Helena was the only person on the scene advertising herself as an S&M model. All the other women, ranging in age from nineteen to fifty-eight, were just out for kicks. We eliminated all those slaves searching only for mistresses as well as those whose stated preference was to be dominated by a couple. We then discarded all those new to the scene. That left us with about 300 ads, still far too many. We then decided to rule out others on geographical grounds and so deleted ads posted by people based in the south, given that Helena lived in the north-eastern town of Varese and had been kidnapped in Turin. Sorting them by region, we realized that the majority of slaves lived in Lombardy, Piedmont, or the Veneto, and were concentrated in the major cities. Max noticed that on a couple of occasions the same ad cropped up twice, days or weeks apart. And it was while we were checking this out that I spotted a familiar nickname: Barbie Slave.

'That's the slave-name of Antonina Gattuso, Giraldi's girlfriend.'

'Are you certain?' Max asked in astonishment.

'Absolutely. The poem I saw in Giraldi's photo album was signed Barbie Slave.'

'Well, it would appear that Giraldi's slave is not all that faithful.'

'Not necessarily. She told me that sometimes Giraldi forces her to submit to other masters as a form of punishment when she's misbehaved. Look, that's just what the ad says. "My name's Barbie. I'm a thirty-five year-old slave. I'm good-looking and expert, but sometimes a little disobedient. To punish me, my master subjects me to intense and no-holds-barred punishment by other masters, on condition that he is present. My master will select the successful applicants, who must all be expert, sophisticated and imaginative." '

Max turned to Ivaz and Arakno. 'Maybe we've found what we're looking for.'

The two guys returned to work. After about fifteen minutes, they informed us that the password consisted of a sequence of numbers and letters and that it would take a while to crack.

'I'll go and make coffee,' Max said.

I followed him into his kitchen. From the ceiling hung all sorts of pans and from the wall-racks the strangest-looking cooking utensils. It was the only neat and tidy room in the house.

'Have you heard from Virna?' Max asked, lighting the ring.

'She's switched off her cellphone.'

'I imagine she'll come back with a final decision.'

'I reckon so too. And I'm not optimistic.'

'It's not as if you've made much of an effort to meet her halfway.'

I lit a cigarette. 'I can drink less but I can't just jack in this work.'

'The club's doing okay; you could settle for that.'

'Are you serious?'

'Of course not. But then you have to give it to her straight. Have you ever explained to her what it really is that drives you to go getting yourself in trouble?'

'I'm not sure I know myself.'

Max set out the coffee cups. 'Haven't you admitted to yourself that the reason you work as an unlicensed investigator is because you're longing for justice, the justice the courts denied you?'

'Give me a break, Max. Don't play the shrink with me.'

'Okay, Marco. But you know I'm right. And you should tell Virna, too, otherwise you'll lose her for good.'

'It's a risk I have to run.'

'Well, do as you like. It just means Old Rossini and I will have to cheer you up.'

His tone had annoyed me, making me want to pick a quarrel, but Ivaz appeared at the door. 'We've nailed it,' he said with a grin.

Antonina Gattuso was the tidy sort. She had never deleted anything and all her emails were filed away in folders. One folder was of particular interest, since it contained all Antonina's correspondence with a certain 'Docile Woman', who, a little while after Helena's kidnapping, had written to Barbie Slave saying: 'I'm scared. They're getting more and more demanding and insistent. I'm running out of excuses for my husband about being away from home. And anyway we've got to find out what happened to Helena. Why did they take her? And where to? This has never happened before. I'm supposed to meet them the day after tomorrow. I've tried postponing it but they wouldn't let me. Master Mariano has got to intervene ... '

'Have you got the replies?'

'Sure,' Arakno said. 'They're all right here.'

Barbie Slave had replied the same evening. 'Keep calm. Master Mariano is looking for a solution and, in any case, it's important they don't realize that you know about Helena. It could be dangerous. Behave the same as always and nothing will happen to you.'

Docile Woman had written back a couple of days later: 'I met up with them. I was absolutely terrified but everything was just as usual. I got home late and my husband made a scene. He suspects I have a lover. I can't go on like this . . . '

Barbie Slave had replied: 'This situation is difficult for all of us, and for Master Mariano more than anyone else. Like me, you're just a slave; you count for nothing. Try to smoothe things over with your husband. He mustn't have any suspicions. Master Mariano is addressing the situation and we just have to trust him.'

Three days later Docile Woman sent another email: 'Helena's disappearance was on the TV. They think she's gone back to Germany. So what did Master Mariano tell the police? What happens if the police find out whose hands she's really in?'

Barbie Slave: 'The police neither know nor imagine anything. Don't panic.'

Docile Woman: 'They've got back in touch. I have to meet them next week. I'm frightened.'

Barbie Slave: 'Master Mariano has hired some people with links to organized crime to trace Helena. When they find her, all our problems will be sorted. The Master of Knots will be out of our lives for good.'

I turned to look at Max. 'The rope rose must be the handiwork of this Master of Knots. Giraldi, that piece of shit, has been taking us for idiots.'

'Then he made a serious mistake. Beniamino warned him.'

'Master of Knots . . . ring any bells?'

'No. Perhaps it's some kind of title in the S and M pecking order. Whatever it is, we'll soon find out from Giraldi.'

'It'll be the first time we've ever had to knock a client about to obtain information.'

'Right. He's convinced he's dealing with a bunch of morons. Just look at the last message his girlfriend sent; "Today I met one of the people who's looking for Helena. He asked me a whole lot of questions. Master Mariano has a plan to lead them in the direction of the Master of Knots . . ."'

'What a total bastard!' I exploded.

Max asked his Sardinian friends to break into Docile Woman's inbox. The password was straightforward and they only took a couple of minutes. There was just one message, sent by someone called Master Sade. 'Thursday, 6 p.m., usual place.'

'We'll be there too,' Max said. 'But right now I'd like to see Master Sade's correspondence.'

Over an hour later, Arakno announced: 'There's nothing there – a total waste of time. He's erased everything.'

I called Rossini and invited him to the cinema, our code for urgent meetings. Max paid the hackers and agreed on an arrangement whereby we could contact them for further assistance, were it to prove necessary. Then he drove them to the airport.

I went back next door to my own flat. I had forgotten to close the shutters and the entire flat was now suffocatingly hot, so I switched on the air-conditioning and poured myself two fingers of Calvados. I was furious. Giraldi had to be desperate to concoct a plan of such stupidity. His real aim was not to get his wife back but to extricate himself from the clutches of the Master of Knots and his accomplices. Otherwise, he'd have told us about the gang right away. He knew Helena would not be coming back and, after his conversation with Avvocato Bonotto, he had realized that we might be the solution to all his troubles, as well as the instrument of his vengeance. 'People with links to organized crime', as Antonina Gattuso had described us in her email to Docile Woman. There was a lot that was still unclear, though. Above all, how Giraldi was planning to set us on the kidnappers' trail and just what kind of denouement he had in mind. Maybe he was hoping we'd physically eliminate the bad guys; it was the only way he could be sure of keeping the cops off his case. I poured myself some more Calvados and stopped racking my brains. I'd have all the answers I needed soon enough.

Old Rossini smoked in silence as he listened to my account, a conceited grin playing on his lips. 'I might remind you that I told you right at the start we shouldn't take this case, but I don't want to rub it in.'

'Well, now we can drop it,' I teased him. 'After all, we've already had our fees.'

'No, no. I warned him not to try fucking us over. I want to teach him how to behave as well as find out everything he's been hiding from us. Then, okay, maybe we can forget about the whole thing.'

It was my turn to grin. He pretended not to notice and changed the subject, spitefully asking me if I'd heard from Virna.

'Sure. We're getting married next month.'

'I get the picture. She's dumping you again.'

'So? Why should I worry? Max says the two of you will be on hand to cheer me up.'

'Max made a mistake trying to speak on my behalf. I'm telling you: the instant she dumps you, I'm vanishing till you're over it. With a broken heart, you're downright insufferable.'

'This whole thing is such a pain.'

'You're the pain. If things aren't working out with Virna,

move on and find yourself another woman. You're not a kid any more.'

'That's not how it works.'

'Oh yes it is. The problem is, you're an entire generation of whingers. For you lot, life is just constant sorrow.'

I told him to go to hell and went and took a shower. By the time I emerged, Max had already returned and was talking the case over with Old Rossini.

'We were thinking of leaving right away for Varese,' Max said.

'Yeah, I agree.'

'Beniamino suggests we drop the case once we've clarified the situation with the client.'

'And what do you think?'

Max ran a hand over his prominent paunch. 'I don't know. It depends what Giraldi tells us happened to his wife. As I said before, I don't want this stuff weighing on my conscience.'

I pulled my cigarettes out of my shirt pocket. 'Right. It's too soon to take a decision either way.'

Halfway to Varese, Max made another attempt to draw us into a conversation about prison. 'Looking at all those S and M websites, seeing all those photos of people strapped to their beds, I kept thinking about new prisoners just transferred from criminal-insane asylums,' he said. 'Their wrists and ankles still bore the marks of the restraint-bed belts. They'd been held naked, with a hole in the mattress to shit and piss through, and administered horse injections twice a day. They had this lost look about them, and nobody wanted them in their cell. Do you remember those guys?'

Beniamino and I glanced at each other in silence. The old gangster was driving fast, never budging from the overtaking lane. I lit another cigarette while Max continued, oblivious.

'Every jail has a couple of cells set aside for rejects: the insane, the HIV-positive, drug-addicts who are still injecting, and guys who are plain ill. Even the screws feel disgusted and don't want to go anywhere near them. When they're told to do a cell-search, they draw straws. Now I think of it, do you guys remember the searches, when the Carabinieri were sent in with shields and batons? They would cram us all in the showers so tight we couldn't breathe, and then when we were let back to our cells we'd find all our stuff on the floor: coffee, salt, cooking oil and jam all over our clothes, our letters and postcards all ripped up. And we had to keep quiet about it, otherwise they'd kick our heads in and we'd wind up in an isolation cell. Isolation, another right fucking drag . . . When I think of all the time we spent in isolation straight after being arrested, before the investigators got round to questioning us and sending us to the main block with all the others . . .'

Rossini cleared his throat. 'I did fifteen years in prison and Marco did seven. Of the three of us, you've spent the least time inside. In fact, your stay was far too brief for you to be breaking our balls with this crap.'

'What the fuck do you mean? I'm bottom of the class and so have no right to speak?'

'That's right, Max. But that's not all. You spent almost your whole time in Rebibbia, the cushiest jail in Italy. You had privileges. Me and Marco, on the other hand, were in some shitholes you can't even begin to imagine.'

'True enough,' Max conceded. 'But I've seen enough to know what prison is like . . .'

'In that case, quit talking about it,' I snapped.

'I've already told you. All this S and M stuff has unlocked some memories. It's making me feel uneasy.'

'Your fucking problem,' Beniamino said, closing it off.

The neighbourhood dogs caught our scent and started to bark – Giraldi's Argentine Dog was the fiercest. His house was dark and silent and when I rang the doorbell, nobody answered. Giraldi's Mercedes was missing.

'Hurry up and get back in the car,' Rossini said. 'The dogs are making too much of a din; any minute now the lights will all go on.'

'It's two in the morning,' I remarked. 'Where the hell has he gone?'

'Maybe he's busy giving his sex slave a training session,' Max interjected acidly. 'Try and get him on his cellphone.'

I dialled the number. 'Unobtainable.'

'Get in,' Rossini said, turning the ignition key. 'We'll come back later.'

We spent a couple of hours at a nightclub where Beniamino was a regular patron. While he chatted with some people he knew, Max and I sat at the bar. In a matter of seconds, two hostesses came over.

'We're with him,' I said, pointing to Beniamino.

The two girls disappeared as fast as they'd arrived; there was no hope of fleecing us.

'Nice-looking girls, though,' I said, as I watched them walk away.

'They're not our type. We're from different planets.'

'You never know. If they find the right man and another way of living, they're only too happy to jack it in. It's the dream of every girl starting out in the nightclubs.'

'Would you want to date a nightclub hostess?'

I shrugged. 'If she was anything like Sylvie, I'd jump at the chance.'

Max smiled. 'You're treading on dangerous ground.'

'Not at all. I fancy her, that's all.'

'More than Virna?'

'No. Besides, I love Virna.'

'I've met a woman,' Max suddenly told me.

'About time.'

'I met her in Padova at a squat run by anti-globalization activists. I like her a lot, but she's vegetarian.'

'That's not too serious.'

'No, I know. I want to invite her to dinner, but I can't work out the menu.'

'Take her to a restaurant.'

'I prefer playing at home.'

'You're a complicated man, Max.'

'Look who's talking.'

Beniamino walked over to us with a satisfied smile on his face. 'Coming here was a great idea. I've just closed a really good deal.'

'More lire to dig up before the euro comes in?' I asked.

'No, no. An old acquaintance is looking for a yacht for some Eastern European purchasers who are prepared to pay good money.'

'And I bet you know just where to lay your hands on such a thing.'

'Naturally. There's this guy who's made a packet exploiting Chinese workers in illegal sweatshops, and he's just bought himself a yacht. I figure he's in for a nasty surprise.'

'Sounds risky to me.'

'There's no such thing as a safe job,' he snorted. 'A professional, like yours truly, plans things down to the millimetre. It's the only way to avoid handcuffs. Besides, all I've got to do is deliver the yacht somewhere on the Croatian coast. The rest is up to the purchasers.'

'Why don't you go back to holding up banks?' Max joked. 'You could start with one that finances the arms trade – I can give you a whole list to choose from.'

'Too many risks for too little money,' Rossini replied seriously.

Giraldi still hadn't arrived home, so we drove back into Varese and popped into a bar near the covered market. It was six a.m. and the place was full of stallkeepers, hauliers and immigrant market porters stuffing themselves with sandwiches, beer and spiked coffee. Max was almost the only person ordering a cappuccino and a croissant. The bar was hot and reeked of smoke, sweat and hard work. I tried again to call Giraldi but his cellphone was still switched off, so I asked the barman for the phone book. If I didn't find Giraldi by eight, I was going to phone Antonina Gattuso. We had to force her to disclose Docile Woman's identity so we could turn up at the appointment she had fixed with Helena's kidnappers. As there wasn't a single Gattuso in the book, I looked for her husband's name, Cavedoni. Fortunately, there was just one.

'Who knows where the hell Giraldi has got to,' Max grumbled.

'There's not much we do know about the guy. Maybe he's at his mum's,' Beniamino joked.

I phoned him every twenty minutes, then at eight on the dot I punched in Cavedoni's number. Beniamino stopped me. 'It would be wiser to make the call from a phone box.'

I found one right across the street from the bar. As I inserted my phonecard, I couldn't help noticing that it carried an ad for the Carabinieri, celebrating the one hundredth anniversary of the force's foundation. On the second ring, a man's voice answered the phone.

'I want to speak with Antonina.'

'Antonina? She isn't here. She didn't come home last night,' the man replied, sounding worried. He then started to assail me with a string of questions. 'Who are you, anyway? How come you're looking for my wife at eight o'clock in the morning?'

I gently replaced the receiver on its hook. So Master Mariano and Barbie Slave had vanished. It could hardly be a coincidence. Perhaps they'd run off together. But that made no sense – Antonina had a daughter and a husband, while Giraldi had his business plus a kidnapped wife. One thing was certain. If they didn't surface within the next few hours, the police would intervene.

'Let's go home,' Rossini said. 'There's nothing more we can do round here.'

As we drove home to Padova, we went back over the case in some detail. Both logic and experience led us to suppose that the Master of Knots was the reason for the disappearance of Giraldi and Antonina. Giraldi must have blurted out something that had alarmed the kidnappers, and then, without wasting any time, they had moved to neutralize any danger that Master Mariano and his sex slave might represent. If this theory was right, Giraldi and Antonina might have told the kidnappers they'd engaged us to look for Helena. In which case they'd now know the address of my club, La Cuccia. We were going to have to keep our eyes open.

News of the disappearance of Antonina Gattuso, the wife of Silvio Cavedoni, appeared in the newspapers two days later. The stories reported the astonishment of her husband, close family and work colleagues. Antonina was described as a woman devoted to her family and to her work; in an interview in a local daily paper, her parish priest praised her for her social commitment. On TV, the missing-persons slot did a long report on her disappearance and her husband appealed for witnesses. Her daughter wrote a letter with the heading 'Mummy come home'. The Carabinieri captain heading up the investigation let it be known they were working on the theory that she had vanished deliberately. The only thing they knew for sure was that on the day of her disappearance Antonina had left work in her own car.

No mention whatever was made of Giraldi, whose brother reported his disappearance a full two weeks later, by which time everybody had already given up worrying about Antonina. The delay in reporting Giraldi's disappearance was justified by the firm belief that he'd gone to Germany to search for his wife, and it wasn't until the companies for which Giraldi worked as a rep began to complain of his absence that Ettore Giraldi became concerned. All it then took was a quick phone call to Helena's family in Germany to establish that neither of them had turned up there.

Press and TV treated Giraldi's disappearance with their customary indifference. As a news item, it soon sank without trace, and it never occurred to anybody to link the two disappearances. Besides, loads of people disappear every day in Italy and a fair percentage of them are never seen again. Max researched the issue thoroughly on the internet and discovered that unless a child is involved or there is a well-founded suspicion of foul play, investigations into disappearances never go much beyond routine procedures.

Nothing much out of the ordinary happened at the club, except that a couple of Albanians turned up asking for protection money. Old Rossini went and had a word with their boss and the matter was resolved without anyone getting hurt. From the evidence, we were convinced that Master Mariano and his Barbie Slave had been eliminated. As far as we were concerned, the case of Helena's kidnapping was now closed. We had been paid handsomely and had done very little to earn it. Out of a sense of professional thoroughness, Max sent a message to Docile Woman.

'We are aware that you are a victim of the Master of Knots. As you will know, he and his gang are responsible for the disappearance of three people. We believe that you too may be in danger. We can help you.'

71

That afternoon the heat was particularly oppressive. I was stretched out on the sofa with the shutters closed and the air-conditioning turned up high, thinking about Virna. She had been back for several days now but hadn't wanted to see me. We'd had a pretty stormy phone conversation during which she had said that our relationship wasn't going to work. Each of us was too grown-up just to fit in round the other's demands. I had seen it coming but was upset anyway. I needed a woman. I needed her. And I was dying for a fuck. I hadn't said anything about it to my associates, and I wasn't planning to. They'd have morphed into a pair of attentive mother-hens, burying me in kindnesses and counselling, without of course missing the opportunity to say, 'We told you so.' Max rapped at the door.

'Am I disturbing you?'

'No. I was just pondering my prolonged period of sexual inactivity.'

'A great topic for daytime TV,' Max said sympathetically. 'Listen. There's a development in the Helena Heintze case.'

'Go on.'

'Docile Woman has replied to our message and wants to meet us. Tomorrow, 5.30 in the afternoon, at Milan Central Station, opposite the pharmacy.'

'And how will we recognize her?'

'She'll approach us.'

'What, the newspaper-under-the-arm routine?'

'An interior-design glossy, actually. If she feels in any way uneasy, she'll turn on her heels and we'll never spot her.'

'We'd better hope she likes the look of us.'

'Heard from Rossini?'

'He's on his way over to Croatia with the stolen yacht and won't be back for a couple of days.'

'Right. So we'll go tomorrow, just the two of us.'

'Let's hope it's not a trap.'

'There's no risk of that. That time of day the place is heaving. Docile Woman has chosen it in compliance with the security guidelines that S and M sites recommend.'

Max went off to yet another of his fair-trade association meetings and I dumped myself back on the couch. Johnny Winter welcomed me, singing, 'Don't take advantage of me.' I stopped contemplating my broken heart and focused instead on the unforeseen development in the case. Docile Woman had decided to take up our suggestion. Her situation must have become unbearable. I fell asleep thinking about Antonina Gattuso. Her husband was the only one still looking for her. Every week he made an appeal on the missing-persons slot on TV. He addressed his wife directly. He suspected she had run away from him and from their little girl, from their rented flat and their Saturdays at the shopping mall. If he'd had any inkling of the double life his beloved Antonina had been leading, he wouldn't have wasted his breath.

We left for Milan late morning, not wanting to run the risk of arriving late. The temperature hadn't dropped a single degree. I'd left my Skoda in the sun and Max, the moment his backside touched the scalding seat, unleashed a torrent of unkind comments regarding my mental faculties. He'd stopped at a newsagents and as well as the interior-design magazine, he'd bought several newspapers. He started to flick through them, commenting on the stories as he went.

'On the twentieth of July, in Genoa, there's going to be a summit meeting of "the world's most powerful leaders". Did you know that?'

'Yeah. It seems they're throwing a ring of steel round the city to stop your lot from busting everyone's balls.'

'Right. Well, I was just considering the possibility of going on the demonstration.'

'The heat must have melted your brain, Max. You know you're living on a razor's edge. All you've got to do is sneeze at a cop and you'll be straight back behind bars.'

'There are going to be tens of thousands of people there. Besides, I'd stick with the fair-trade contingent. They're total pacifists.'

'What the fuck are you talking about? One group of

protesters has announced on TV that it aims to invade the prohibited zone.'

'The red zone.'

'Whatever. So there are bound to be clashes with the police.'

'But I'll be in the other section of the demonstration.'

'Have you forgotten what happened in March, at the last summit, in Naples?' I spluttered. 'The cops broke the heads of everyone who came within striking range; they didn't stop to ask which part of the movement you belonged to. And that was when we had a Centre-Left government. Just think what'll happen now the Right's back in power.'

'The Genoa Social Forum has asked for assurances and is in talks with the Ministry of the Interior. There's not going to be any trouble.'

'You're not going to fall for that bullshit, I hope. Why don't you just say you've already made your mind up?'

'I said I'm thinking about it.'

'Do what the fuck you like, Max, just don't ask for my blessing.'

Silence fell, heavy with tension. After a little while, Fat Max started commenting on the news items again. Then he folded the paper and shoved an article in front of me. 'Take a look at this.'

'I'm driving, for Christ's sake.'

' "Silent crimes," ' Max read. ' "Failing prison healthcare kills inmates . . ." '

'Max, for God's sake, don't start going on about prison again.'

'The list's quite short. Just those who've died this year. A fifty-nine-year old, in Enna city prison. He croaked on the very morning they informed him he was going to be released on health grounds. In Milan prison, a chronically

75

sick prisoner died from an embolism. He had applied to be transferred to an external unit. In Palermo, another poor bastard died after an operation performed in the prison hospital. They'd left a tube in his guts...'

'That doesn't only happen in prison,' I butted in.

'Anyway, he died ... Then at Prato a nurse is under investigation. It's alleged she failed to assist a Spanish prisoner who was having a heart attack. He was forty-five. In Vigevano, a sixty-year-old prisoner died, again, of an embolism. The prison doctors hadn't arranged for him to be hospitalized.'

'Cut it out, Max.'

'Listen to this. In Padova, prison doctors thought a detainee had faked a heart attack until he had a second one, which killed him. Again in Padova, a North African prisoner died following a hunger strike. He had lost twenty kilos but nobody took the trouble to provide him with the obligatory healthcare that the judge had ordered. I'll spare you the suicides, which are on the increase. Still, there is one piece of good news. The government has earmarked 830 billion lire for the construction of twenty-two new prisons.'

'Have you finished?'

'Yes, I have. How many people did we see die inside?'

'People don't give a shit about what happens in prison.'

'Not even you.'

'Not much, no. When you're behind bars, all you think about is how to get out as fast as you can, without too much damage. And once you're free, all you want to do is forget. You don't give a fuck about the others. Everyone looks out for number one.'

'I don't want to forget.'

'More fool you. It makes no difference anyway; prison conditions in Italy can only get worse.'

'That's not a reason.'

'I'll tell you a story, Max. One day a child rapist was brought in, and they placed him in isolation till the public prosecutor was ready to question him. He was scared out of his wits because the Carabinieri had explained what happens in prison to people like him. The screws went to work on him too, and in the end he ripped up a sheet to make himself a length of rope, tied one end to the bars of his window and placed the noose around his neck. Thing is, he didn't have the guts to jump off the stool. So two guards opened his cell door and went inside to help him hang himself. One kicked the stool away and the other grabbed hold of his legs and yanked.'

'How do you know that's what happened?'

'Because I saw the whole thing. I was in the cell opposite his. When I was questioned about it, I said that when the two screws opened the guy's cell door, he was already swinging from the bars.'

'Fuck it, Marco. How could you?'

'What would you have had me do? Nobody would have believed me and every screw in every fucking jail in Italy would have felt duty-bound to bust my arse.'

'What you've described was an execution, God damn it, and they got away with it . . .' Max stuttered, indignant.

'Same as they always do. Now get off my case, will you?'

Docile Woman had chosen the right place to meet. At five thirty in the afternoon, Milan Central Station was far too crowded for us to see if anyone had us under surveillance. Max went and stood outside the pharmacy and pretended to read his interior-design magazine. I went and stood over by a huge newsagent's and pretended to be interested in the magazines. I couldn't help noticing the vast array of stuff

77

aimed at collectors. Every week, you could buy miniature soldiers, statuettes for your Christmas crib, toy cars and a whole lot of other exclusively plastic knick-knacks with which to fill your lounge. 'People really are going out of their minds,' I said to myself as I shifted my gaze to the porn section. There was even one exclusively devoted to arses. I hoped Docile Woman wouldn't take too long.

Fortunately, having looked Max up and down for a good ten minutes, she decided to trust him and stepped forward. Max shook hands with her and then gestured in my direction. I walked over and she greeted me with a nod of her head. 'Follow me,' she said, as she walked over to the down escalator. On reaching street level, she walked out of the station, turned left, crossed the road and entered a bar.

We sat in a small, empty room and ordered drinks. She was in her early forties, slim and elegant-looking, and her face was interesting rather than pretty, with large, hazel eyes. She must have been loaded, because her suit, bag and sandals were all designer. She was wearing diamond and white-gold earrings and had a wedding ring on her finger.

'No names,' she said straight away.

'Agreed.'

'How did you find me?'

'We hacked into Barbie Slave's inbox and read the messages you sent each other.'

I pulled the rope flower out of my pocket and she looked at it. 'The Master of Knots,' she whispered, looking round. 'Where did you find it?'

'Giraldi found it in the hotel room where Helena was kidnapped.'

'And now he's disappeared too. Everybody's disappeared,' she said, clearly distressed. Her face contracted to a grimace. She was on the verge of breaking down but managed to control herself, taking a couple of deep breaths. 'You can't imagine what I've been through.'

'It might be an idea if you told us the whole story, right from the start,' Max said by way of encouragement.

She took a sip of cold coffee and began to speak. She had met Helena through her work in the fashion industry and had been attracted to her at once. Till then, she had never had the courage to confront her bisexuality, but the German woman had unleashed in her the longing to make love to a woman. Helena was happy to have an admirer. One evening, after a fashion show, Helena and her husband had invited her out to dinner. Giraldi started talking about S&M and then invited her to follow them home. After a moment's initial embarrassment, she told them she wasn't interested either in being dominated or in having sex with a couple. Giraldi then offered to train her as a mistress. He would restrict himself to watching. She was in two minds but Helena kept looking at her longingly, so she accepted the offer.

That was the first and last time she made love with the German woman. Giraldi introduced her to Antonina Gattuso and so it was with Antonina that Docile Woman learnt the art of domination. Barbie Slave, however, was not nearly as attractive as Helena, so Docile Woman placed an ad at a website that Giraldi recommended. Quite a number of women replied. She met them all but had (rather unsatisfactory) sex with just one of them. Then she met Cristiana, a twenty-four-year-old who exuded sensuality from every pore. They met three times, in three different hotels in Milan.

At their fourth appointment, instead of Cristiana, a tall, dark, dodgy-looking man in his fifties turned up. To persuade her to enter the hotel room, he told her he was

Cristiana's father. He took a videotape out of his jacket, insisted she watch it, and then talked of blackmail. He showed her a list of people who would receive copies of the video showing her dominating Cristiana, and the first name on the list was her husband's. Then came her close family, work colleagues and, finally, her neighbours. She felt lost. Not giving in to blackmail would have meant total ruin, so she asked the man how much money he wanted. He shook his head and said that a person's reputation was without price. Then he told her what she had to do to buy his silence. She felt crushed, and racked her brains for some other way out but was forced to surrender. She had no other choice. Just like Cristiana, who had fallen victim to the same loathsome blackmail.

The blackmailer made a phone call and a little later two men knocked on the door. One was young and had a gym-sculpted body, and the other was older and skinny. The skinny one took a video camera out of a bag while the younger one took his clothes off. They made her wear a leather mask, tied her to the bed and that was how she made her first S&M video. All this had happened a year and a half ago. Since then she had met the rest of the Bang Gang, as they liked to call themselves. There were six of them altogether. She had never seen the gang leader's face, as he never turned up until she had been blindfolded. The others referred to him respectfully as the Master of Knots since, as they explained to her, he was a follower of Chimuo Nureki, the Sensei of Kinbiken, the ancient Japanese art of bondage. It was the Master of Knots who took personal charge of tying her up and who directed the filming.

The other participants varied according to the plot of the film. She had become their slave, in the true sense of the word. They could do whatever they liked with her, even if they always took great care to guarantee her anonymity, making her wear a mask, and not overstepping the limits. They forced her to invite Antonina Gattuso to a hotel room, where there was a hidden camera. Antonina had showed up with Giraldi. Then, once Giraldi had also fallen victim to blackmail, they forced him to involve his wife.

'So, when Helena was kidnapped, did Giraldi realize he was going to meet the Master of Knots and his gang?'

'I don't know. It must have been a first appointment, given that it was at a hotel. Usually the gang picked me up from a bus stop in Corso Sempione. They made me wear a pair of glasses with painted lenses and took me to a specially kitted-out basement flat in some villa or apartment building.'

'Here in Milan?'

'Yes. The journey took fifteen to twenty minutes.'

'If I've understood you correctly, the gang uses blackmail to force women into taking part in pornographic films for the illegal market.'

'Yes. But the way they see it, it's not just business – those pigs get off on it. As for the Master of Knots, he's a kind of spiritual leader to them. He never stops talking about the principles of Japanese sadomasochism and his Sensei.'

'Could you explain that?'

'In Japan, sadomasochism isn't about mutual pleasure. It's about power, absolute domination over women who, according to these bastards, nowadays possess far too much power within society.'

'How many women were involved?'

'I've no idea. I only made videos with Cristiana and Antonina.'

'Why do you think they kidnapped Helena?'

She took a cigarette from my packet. 'I don't know. But

I've thought about this so much that I've developed a hunch.'

'Tell us what it is.'

'Helena was incredibly beautiful – she had the perfect body. You wouldn't find many slaves to compare with her. I reckon they kidnapped her to make a whole series of videos, each one more violent than the last.'

'You're assuming they tortured her to death.'

'Yes, I am. The most sought-after videos are those in which women are tortured by over-dilating their anuses and vaginas. With me, Antonina and Cristiana, the gang used small objects to avoid tissue lacerations that we couldn't have explained to our husbands. But I think they probably fist-fucked Helena to death.'

Max and I glanced at one another. Fist-fucking, with the insertion of a hand into the vagina or anus, had to be a highly dangerous practice, and a hideous way to die.

'So, in other words,' Max asked, 'you think this gang has graduated to killing people, right?'

'I do. The fact is that, despite their exorbitant expense, there's a vast demand for snuff videos.'

'There's one thing I don't understand,' I said. 'If this was Helena and Giraldi's first appointment with them, why did the gang organize the kidnapping? Up until this point, they'd done things differently, using a hidden camera to set up the blackmail.'

'That's true. I'm convinced it was Antonina who told them about Helena's work as an S and M model. Maybe she even got some photos for them or gave the gang Helena's address. She detested Giraldi's wife, and wanted Master Mariano all to herself. When she phoned me to say that Helena had been kidnapped, she was euphoric.'

'What about Giraldi's and Antonina's disappearance? Have you got a hunch about that too?'

'They must have made a bad move.'

'There's another thing I don't get,' I said. 'Why didn't they make Giraldi disappear along with his wife?'

This time it was Max who replied. 'The only plausible explanation is that they weren't intending to kill Helena. They kidnapped her in order to have her available for use in more violent videos, and she must have died by accident, at which point they would have been forced to eliminate Mariano and his girlfriend as potentially dangerous witnesses.'

'You're going to have to be careful,' I warned the woman. 'If they contact you again, tell us at once. We'll see you're protected.'

'I don't think I'll be hearing from them again,' she replied. 'As far as they're concerned, I'm no threat. You're the only people I've told this story – except for my analyst of course – because I know you won't run around blabbing about it. Antonina told me you were gangsters or something.'

'So your reputation matters more to you than the life of three people, does it?' Max asked. He resented being called a gangster.

I stared at Max to shut him up but Docile Woman had taken no offence. 'You bet it does,' she replied. 'I now have the chance to start living again, whereas if I go to the police, my only choice will be between suicide or the convent . . .'

Max was about to hit back, but I beat him to it. 'Is there anything you can tell us that might help identify the gang members?'

She took a sheet of paper from her bag. 'This is a list of the nicknames they used to contact me.'

'Didn't they ever call each other by name?'

'Never. But I am sure of one thing: they're all Italians, and Northern Italians at that.'

'Including the Master of Knots?'

'Yes. He had a deep voice and a distinct Milanese accent.'

'Do you happen to remember the numberplate of the car that used to pick you up?'

She shook her head. 'No, I'm afraid I never noticed. If it's any use, the car was a dark green Lancia Y ten.'

Max took a small notebook and a pen out of his pocket. 'Would you mind describing the various members of the Bang Gang whom you personally saw – even the tiniest detail may prove useful.'

About half an hour later, looking pale and tired, the woman left. She had clearly found it hard to go back over everything she had had to live through since first meeting Cristiana. Max ordered his third iced tea, while I had a rum and Coke.

'Vile business. Let's hope she's got a good analyst.'

'We've absolutely got to find a way of stopping the Master of Knots and his gang,' Max said angrily.

'The only person who can do that is Rossini. With lead.'

'Right.'

'Assuming he feels like it; you know what he's like. He has concerns about his reputation.'

'I'm sure that once we've explained to him the nature of the Master of Knots' activities he'll be only too pleased to help.'

'Maybe. But we still have very little to go on, and by now the Bang Gang has probably moved to another part of the country.'

'But it won't have changed the nature of its activities. You heard what Docile Woman said: to these people, sadomasochism isn't just a business.'

'It still won't be easy to find them.'

'We have to keep monitoring the website ads. The moment the gang surfaces, using any of the nicknames the woman gave us, we'll be all over them.'

'I've got another idea: we investigate the illegal porn market.'

'Do we know anyone?'

'An old prison acquaintance. If Rossini has a word with him, I think he'll be able to help us.'

Old Rossini walked back into the club three days later, rather more tanned than usual and with a new, expensive-looking watch on his wrist. His business trip to Croatia had clearly gone well. He ordered a Kir Royale – champagne and crème de cassis.

'I've never seen you drink that concoction before,' I said.

'Every now and then I like a change.'

'We've got some news,' Max announced, biting into a chocolate.

Rossini looked us straight in the eye. 'I'm in a good mood. I hope it's not to do with that S and M business.'

'That's it.'

'At least let me finish my drink in peace.'

We let him have his way, then Max fetched his notebook and reported what Docile Woman had told us.

Beniamino swore under his breath. A good sign: the old gangster was indignant. Max and I glanced at each other in satisfaction.

'There wasn't all this filth in my day', he said bitterly. 'Pimps were regarded as scum and in prison they had to be kept in isolation, otherwise they'd get knifed in the showers. There are no rules any more, and pieces of shit like this Master of Knots can get away with anything. They haven't

86

got the balls to put their lives on the line or risk imprisonment to earn a decent crust; they'd rather rely on blackmail and violence.'

'All they deserve is a good hiding,' Max said, stringing him along.

'Someone's got to stop them,' I added. 'These people are dangerous as well as crazy.'

Rossini lit a cigarette. 'The Croatian yacht job was lucrative and I've got nothing urgent on at present, so I can focus on chasing these bastards full-time.'

That was that sorted. I told him my idea of looking for leads in the illegal porn business, starting with the guy we had known in prison. Fat Max said he'd continue sifting through email inboxes. We'd start work the following day.

'Okay, I'm going to Sylvie's place,' Beniamino announced.

'Max wants to go to the anti-G8 demonstration in Genoa.'

Rossini remained silent. He picked up his cigarettes and lighter and slipped them into the pocket of his linen jacket. 'It's just bullshit.'

'I've calculated the risks,' Max said.

'There's sure to be trouble,' I hit back. 'You can't go.'

Old Rossini glanced at me. 'Max knows what we think, but it's his decision.'

I shook my head. 'He's going to end up in deep shit.'

Beniamino spread his arms. 'Max is old enough to figure out the risks.' He got a couple of bottles of champagne and an ice-bucket from Rudy and went off to see his woman.

Max picked up his cellphone and called Arakno. 'Get to work,' he said. He then turned on me. 'Why can't you ever mind your own fucking business?'

'Because you're behaving like a total idiot.'

'I'll be fine.'

'I hope you're right.'

Max got up and left, and I stayed behind to chat with some of the customers. As always, at the end of his gig Maurizio Camardi strolled over and sat down at my table. He told me about a group called La Moranera, which was doing some benefit gigs for a well-digging project in Africa.

'Talk to Rudy,' I said. 'He's the landlord.'

The saxophonist smiled. 'He said you were his musical advisor.'

'Fine, then. Whenever they like.'

Every time the door opened, I glanced up with feigned indifference in the hope of seeing Virna walk in. Rationally, I knew it was all over and I'd lost her for good, but deep down I still couldn't accept it. When the last client had left, Rudy and I took a look at the books. Profits were well up and Rudy gave himself a rise on the strength of it. I gestured over to the Kurdish lad, an illegal immigrant, who was mopping the floor. 'Give him a bit more money. We can afford it.'

'All right.'

'What do you know about him?'

'Almost nothing.'

'See what you can find out. Maybe there's some way we can help him.'

Beniamino stopped by to pick me up towards evening. He had made inquiries into the whereabouts of the porn trafficker we were looking for, but first he wanted a word with Max.

'Look, I've heard some rumours,' he said. 'It appears someone's recruiting hotheads from among Veneto's local football-hooligan community to take to Genoa.'

'There are so many stories doing the rounds right now,' Max said, brushing it aside.

'This is a reliable source. They say the person doing the recruiting is working for the cops.'

'I'll pass it on,' Max snapped.

We had first met Nicola Mirra in Padova jail. At that time, he was serving a sentence for receiving stolen goods but was widely known to be involved in the illegal porn trade. On Rossini's instigation, he was subjected to a trial before a jury of powerful fellow-prisoners. In his defence, he swore on the heads of his entire family that he had never had anything whatsoever to do with child pornography and that all he did was export hardcore photos and videos to North Africa. He was acquitted on grounds of insufficient evidence and nobody touched a hair on his head. He was now living in Brescia, but the information Rossini had gathered suggested it might be worth taking a look at a wine merchant's in Bergamo where he apparently met his clients. We spotted him through the store window, chattering away to a distinguished-looking man of about sixty. Mirra's appearance had changed since the last time we had seen him. He now wore his hair in a crew-cut and he had lost weight.

Rossini headed straight over to his table and Mirra went white in the face. He knew at once it was him we were looking for.

'We have to talk to you,' Rossini began dryly.

'I'm busy,' Mirra snarled.

'This gentleman's just leaving,' Rossini said, placing a hand on the client's shoulder. 'He can buy your filth some other time.'

Mirra's client, his face scarlet, got up and shuffled out the door.

'What the fuck do you want?' Mirra rasped.

'Information,' I replied.

'Go fuck yourselves. We're not in prison here.'

'I'm just dying to hurt you,' Rossini growled, pitching his cigarette butt into Mirra's glass of white wine.

'What do you want to know?'

'Do you know of anyone producing S and M videos? And I mean hardcore.'

'What, snuff?'

'You got it.'

He gave us a worried look. 'I don't trade in that stuff.'

'Maybe you know someone who does.'

'There's not much of it in circulation and what there is comes in from abroad.'

Rossini got up. 'Sorry to have disturbed you.'

When we got outside I grabbed Rossini's arm. 'Why did you leave? We'd only just started working on him.'

'He was feeding us a whole load of crap. He felt safe in there; he wasn't about to tell us anything useful.'

'I get it. You want to have a little chat with him somewhere more private.'

'Precisely. As soon as he leaves, we'll follow him.'

We entered a bar about thirty metres further up the street, from where we could keep an eye on the door to the wine merchant's. We ordered drinks and settled down for a long wait. Where we were, in the higher and more ancient part of Bergamo, the bars and eateries were all crammed with people trying to escape the heat.

'There's a woman over there who looks like she fancies you,' Rossini informed me.

I looked round discreetly. A brunette of about forty, in a long, low-cut dress, lifted her glass by way of greeting. I smiled back. The side slit in her dress revealed a nicely bronzed thigh. Not bad at all. 'Is it that obvious I want a fuck?' I asked Rossini.

'Maybe she's just drunk.'

I got up from the stool. 'Tell me when that jerk Mirra leaves, okay?'

I went and sat down beside her. 'My name's Marco.'

She held out a hand laden with rings. 'Viviana.'

'You're nice-looking, Viviana.'

'So are you.'

'My friend says maybe you're just drunk.'

She smiled. 'I'm only drinking gin fizz. Solid vitamins.'

Rossini clicked his fingers to regain my attention. Mirra had left the wine merchant's.

'I have to go now,' I said. 'Maybe I'll drop by later.'

She looked at her watch. 'I'll be here for another couple of hours.'

'I hope I'll be back in time.'

'I'm counting on it,' she said. Then she added, 'Just a quickie. Nothing heavy, okay?'

Nicola Mirra walked fast, turning round every now and then just to make quite sure we weren't following him. But the streets were far too crowded for him to spot us. He led us to an empty car park just outside the city walls, and as he opened his car door Beniamino jabbed him in the ribs, then banged his head down on the car roof.

'Get in,' he ordered, opening the rear door.

I climbed in the other side and Mirra sat between us. He had a cut on his forehead. 'I've already told you I know nothing!' he shouted.

Rossini punched him in the testicles. Mirra let out a groan, trying to protect his crotch with his hands, but Rossini elbowed him in the face. Once, twice, then a third time. Blood began to pour from a split lip. Rossini took Mirra's left hand and bent the fingers back till they almost snapped.

'I'm listening!' Rossini yelled.

'All right, all right,' Mirra gasped. 'I've heard there is someone, a new guy, who's producing the videos you're after. But he's not selling them here in Italy. His name's Jay Jacovone, an Italian-American. They say he's connected to the Miami Mafia.'

'Where can we find him?' I asked.

'He lives in Rome. That's all I know.'

Rossini let go of the man's hand. 'If you've fed us a line, I'll be back to finish the job.'

We got out of the car and retraced our steps. 'Why did you have to beat him up? All he needed was a little slap to get him to talk.'

Rossini shrugged. 'He deserved a lot worse than he got.'

'Did you really have to beat him up inside the car? I've got his blood on my sleeve.'

'Get a new shirt and throw that one out. It's ugly, anyway.'

'No way.'

'I guess you're itching to get back to that bar so you can see your new girlfriend?'

'Why not?'

Viviana's seat was empty, so I asked the barman if he knew where she'd gone. He told me she had picked up a guy and left about ten minutes earlier.

When we got back the club was still open, and Max was sitting at my table with a bottle of grappa, some chocolates, and a packet of cigarettes laid out before him. A bitter grimace cut across his face like a scar.

'What's up with you?' I enquired.

'Nothing. I was thinking,' he replied, slurring his words ever so slightly.

'Mental jerk-offs, the speciality of your generation,' Old Rossini said flatly.

Max ignored him. Sometimes Beniamino couldn't bear our weaknesses. We were used to that.

'So what were you thinking about?' I asked Max.

'Just what lousy lives people lead.'

'Nothing new in that.'

'No, but I mean this whole S and M thing.' He poured himself a large shot of grappa. 'I've spent the evening reading the emails of the slaves who posted those ads on the websites. Arakno and Ivaz came up with a mass of passwords. For a lot of these women, the desire to be dominated hides either an inability to accept themselves the way they are, or desperate loneliness, or a longing to escape from the imprisonment of their family, their marriage or their job. They confide in their masters like other people confide in their priests and, little by little, their dominators come to play an absolutely pivotal role in their lives...'

'In their *double* lives, you mean,' Rossini said.

'Sure. One of their lives is so-called normal, a day-to-day existence that fails to satisfy them. And then there's this other clandestine life they can never own up to, but which enables them to keep going, to find an equilibrium and a bit of peace.'

'You're right. It's not only about sex,' I said. 'I realized that when I was talking to Antonina Gattuso.'

'What really struck me was the fact that, on a rough calculation, taking in all the different types and categories of ads, there must be well over thirty thousand sadomasochists in Italy. And that still doesn't account for all those who reply to other people's ads but don't post their own.'

'That's a lot of people.'

'I also took a look at some foreign sites. The figures are even higher in Germany, France and Britain. Even the Swiss aren't far behind.'

I tasted the Alligator that Rudy had mixed for me: seven parts Calvados, three of Drambuie, plenty of ice and a slice of green apple, following the recipe invented by Danilo Argiolas, the guy who runs the Libarium bar in Cagliari. It hadn't yet reached the ideal temperature. 'Some put their trust in religion, others in shrinks . . .'

'Yeah, yeah, and still others like their butts whipped,' Rossini interrupted. 'Just tell me, did you find out anything?'

'No, I didn't,' Max replied. 'But I found rather an interesting ad. Someone calling herself Sherazade is offering her services as an S and M model.'

'Like Helena.'

'Precisely.'

'If she's as beautiful as Helena was, the Master of Knots may well get interested.'

'I've contacted our Sardinian friends and asked them to have a go at cracking the password.'

'We've had a bit of a talk with Mirra.'

Max noticed Old Rossini's satisfied grin. 'I'm betting he got hurt.'

I showed him the stains on my shirt. 'A fair bit. Still, it helped refresh his memory. We've finally got the name of the guy who makes the videos.'

Beniamino passed on what we'd learnt from the porn trafficker.

I broke open a packet of cigarettes. 'We're going to have

to spend some time in Rome, so we'll need a safe flat and someone who's really at home in Rome's gangland.'

'I met someone when I was in Rebibbia,' Max said. 'But I don't know if we could trust him.'

'I'll take care of this,' Rossini said. 'I know the right man – one of the old guard. A guy who every now and then gives me an order for contraband goods.'

I retried my cocktail. It was perfect now. 'There's no point all three of us going. Max should stay here and carry on monitoring the ads and emails.'

My associates agreed; Beniamino and I would leave the next day. There was just enough time to grab a few hours' sleep and pack a bag with clothes and a plentiful supply of cash.

Rossini snorted. 'Damn it. I promised Sylvie I'd take her out on the boat for a couple of days. I'm going to have to find some way of earning her forgiveness.'

Again my thoughts turned to Virna. I was tempted to call her but thought better of it. Maybe when we got back from Rome.

Rossini's contact in Rome turned out to be a man called Toni Marazza. They were about the same age and had first met in the high-security prison on the island of Pianosa. Marazza's real speciality was armed robbery but his advancing years and numerous convictions had forced him to switch to arms-dealing. It was he who kept Rome's gangs supplied with the weaponry they needed, through Beniamino, who procured the machine guns from the former Yugoslav army. These weapons were particularly sought-after for the power of their bullets, which could pierce the armoured plating of supposedly bullet-proof security vans.

We met Marazza at a posh restaurant in the central Prati

district, and once they had performed the civilities customary between gangsters, Rossini explained to Marazza the purpose of our trip to Rome. Marazza appeared happy to help us out and, after a brief negotiation of financial terms, he took us to a small, independently accessible flat, situated in a block not far from Piazza Barberini. Until fairly recently, the premises had been let to a pair of young, high-class prostitutes. Their clientele had included two very assiduous members of parliament, who liked to go there to relax a bit during the pauses in their onerous parliamentary schedules – Montecitorio, Italy's Lower House, was a short walk away. Marazza had bought the flat along with all its furnishings and hadn't yet got round to removing the huge mirrors on the ceilings of the two bedrooms.

The flat was going to cost us two million lire a day. Toni Marazza's assistance in tracking down Jay Jacovone, on the other hand, was free of charge. Marazza and Rossini weren't just of the same generation, they had lived by the same code of honour all their lives. The way Marazza saw it, the elimination of an S&M video producer was almost a moral imperative. We had a couple of hours' rest, then Toni dropped by to pick us up. The hunt was on.

We were traipsing in and out of bars, restaurants and clubs of every description until three in the morning. Toni Marazza shook hands, exchanged pleasantries and asked for information. Nobody knew a thing. Jacovone clearly didn't associate with Rome's underworld. In the end Marazza said we were going to have to look elsewhere. If Jacovone had links with the Miami Mafia, the cops were sure to be apprised of his arrival in Italy.

The following evening we rang the doorbell of an exclusive club just off Via Veneto. Marazza had warned us about the strict dress code so I'd gone out and bought some new shoes, a dark-blue suit and a tie. I felt ridiculous and the shoes pinched, but it was a classy joint. A piano player tinkled away distractedly, dishing out smiles to anyone who came within range. I recognized a lot of faces from television. The tables were laid out in such a way as to allow for discreet conversations, but the bar was lined with professional drinkers. When I asked for an Alligator and explained its composition to the barman, he acted scandalized and sought to dissuade me, recommending other Calvados-based cocktails. After some elegant verbal sparring, I was forced to give in and try his 'Apple Cocktail': Calvados, cider, gin and cognac. I downed it and ordered another one straight away – it really was good.

After a little while, the man Toni was looking for walked in. He was in the company of a woman half his age with a fine body and pretty face spoiled by a pair of ice-cold, calculating eyes. It seemed the man was a middle-ranking official at the Ministry of the Interior, with a career going nowhere and a high standard of living to maintain. Marazza, spruced up like he had to lead his daughter up the aisle, took charge of the introductions. The government man packed the girl off to powder her nose then listened to our request, whispered a figure, and agreed to meet us the following evening. I returned to the bar and knocked back my third Apple Cocktail.

I was woken up the next morning by Beniamino suggesting we went out to do some shopping. I told him to go to hell, turned over and went back to sleep. He returned mid-afternoon, laden with parcels, most of them containing presents for Sylvie. There was one for me too: a solid steel Ronson cigarette lighter, the original 1960s model.

'This way you can stop using those crappy plastic things,' he muttered when I thanked him.

That evening Marazza's government contact arrived punctually. I followed him to the toilets and, once he'd counted the cash, he whispered an address and handed me a colour photocopy of a photograph. We had found Jay Jacovone. I rang Max, who was still busy monitoring the emails of S&M sex slaves, but he hadn't yet turned up anything new.

Jacovone's cover turned out to be a firm that exported Italian wines to the US. Its headquarters were located in an office block in the Flaminio district, where Jacovone was also registered as resident. Wearing my new dark-blue suit, I took the lift up to the wine exporters' offices, pretending I'd got off at the wrong floor. It was a smartly furnished place with large photographs of wine cellars and vineyards hanging on the walls. The company proprietor was not at his desk, but his secretary was very helpful, directing me to the office of the lawyer I had said I was looking for.

'He must have some other place where he copies and stores the cassettes,' Rossini said.

'It's not going to be easy to find. We'll have to tail him.'

In Rome, if you have to tail somebody, the ideal way to do it is on a scooter. You can zip through the traffic and, in the midst of all the other scooters, bikes and mopeds, you're hard to spot. Marazza got us one with a powerful engine. When it came to choosing helmets, Beniamino made a great fuss: they had to be elegant but not eye-catching. When we finally headed for the door, the shop assistant heaved a sigh of relief.

It proved hard to find a place from which we could keep an eye on comings and goings at Jacovone's offices without drawing any attention to ourselves. It wasn't a very long street and there weren't any bars or shops. We noticed however that there was a first-floor apartment for sale almost exactly opposite. We told the janitor we were on our way up to the marriage agency on the third floor.

'They're Eastern European whores, every last one of them,' he warned us. 'They'll only marry you for the residence permit.'

Old Rossini pulled from his pocket a leather wallet containing a set of pick-locks, selected one, inserted it in the lock and opened the door without doing any visible damage. From the kitchen window we had a perfect view of the door we wanted to keep an eye on. After a couple of hours, Rossini pointed me out a parked car – a mustard-coloured Fiat Punto. Inside sat a guy reading a newspaper.

'I noticed it when we got here,' he said. 'It hasn't budged a centimetre.'

'You think Jacovone's under surveillance?'

'Who else?'

'By the cops?'

'Maybe. Anyway, let's keep an eye on them. I don't want to get mixed up in any police investigation.'

Jacovone came out of the building on the dot of one-thirty and climbed into a white Jaguar. We rushed down into the street, grabbed the scooter and got behind him. But we weren't alone; the Fiat was also on his tail. It overtook us and moved in to hug Jacovone's bumpers. It certainly wasn't a professional operation; the Fiat driver kept jerking his car around, clearly afraid he might get separated from his prey. Jacovone was heading out towards Fiumicino. We thought he might be going to the airport, but then he turned off into the car park of a fish restaurant on the seafront. The Punto pulled up a little further down the road.

We went into the restaurant, where Jacovone was sitting talking to a couple of old gentlemen. Spread out on the table before them was a brochure from a wine producer, indicating that it was a straightforward business lunch. We made our way over to a free table not too close to Jacovone, from which we could observe him without being noticed. He was fifty-ish, slim, medium height, with dark eyes and hair. You could tell he was American by the way he dressed – he looked like an extra from an American Mafia movie; yellow short-sleeved shirt, trousers, white moccasins and black silk socks. He wore a gold chain round his neck and a ring set with an emerald on the little finger of his left hand. He came on like a Mafia Boss, waving his arms around like Marlon Brando in *The Godfather*.

I glanced at Rossini, who was playing with the bracelets he wore on his left wrist. His scalps. He'd happily add Jacovone's to his collection.

We ordered an antipasto and a plate of spaghetti each. By the time Jacovone ordered coffee, we were already paying our bill. We got back on our scooter and hid behind an ice-cream kiosk, not wanting to be seen by the character in the Fiat.

'It's cost us trouble and money to track down Jacovone,' Old Rossini hissed, 'and that dickhead is going to foul it all up for us.'

'So what do we do?'

'We're going to have to give up following our little Mafioso here and concentrate on the other guy. We need to find out what he wants.'

After a while, Jay Jacovone left the restaurant and drove back to his office, with the Fiat Punto and Rossini and me on the scooter following in his wake. However, rather than stopping outside Jacovone's office, the Fiat drove on to a dirt-cheap hotel close to Stazione Termini.

All it took was 50,000 lire to get the guy on the desk to supply us with his customer's details, his room number and to forget he'd ever laid eyes on us. The name was Flavio Guarnero, thirty-six years old and living in Turin, where he had been born. Rossini knocked gently on the door of room eleven.

'Who's there?' a voice enquired.

'The guy on reception,' Rossini replied.

As soon as Guarnero caught sight of us he attempted to shut the door again, but Rossini shouldered his way in, knocking the guy to the floor. Guarnero jumped back up and made a grab for the bedside cabinet. Beniamino seized him by the throat and wrenched his arm behind his back, immobilizing him.

'Who are you?' Guarnero asked menacingly. He wasn't scaring anybody. He was plump, with thinning, light-brown hair and pale-blue eyes. I opened the drawer of the bedside cabinet, took out a handgun by its barrel and held it up for my associate to see.

'Nine-millimetre Beretta,' Rossini commented. 'Police-issue.'

I noticed his wallet. 'Right. He's a cop,' I said, taking out his ID. 'Superintendent Flavio Guarnero. Turin City Police.'

He didn't look like a street cop. His physique and clumsiness suggested something sedentary.

'What office do you work in?'

'Immigration control.'

Rossini let go of him. I handed the gun to my associate, and he checked it was loaded before pointing it at Guarnero. 'Sit,' he ordered.

'Are you Jacovone's men?' Guarnero asked, massaging his arm.

'No,' I replied. 'We're film critics and we take the view that the films that bastard makes stink.'

The room was hot, dirty and reeked of sweat. I ransacked the wardrobe, and at the bottom of a suitcase I found a document holder containing photocopies of surveillance reports on Jay Jacovone. One of them, marked FBI, confirmed that Jacovone belonged to the Miami Mafia. He'd been involved in the cocaine business until he had gone against 'family' orders and whacked one of the bosses of their Colombian competition. He'd then been sent into exile in Italy to look after the wine business. Trafficking in S&M videos was his own idea, and he supplied these to illegal American and Canadian markets. The FBI were requesting their Italian colleagues not to hamper Jacovone's activities as he'd recently become one of their most valued collaborators. The information he was supplying would enable them to dismantle the entire Miami drugs cartel.

'Our friend Flavio here is running an unauthorized investigation,' I said. 'Cops don't normally keep confidential files in hotel cupboards.'

'What's your interest in Jacovone?' Rossini asked.

'Fuck yourselves,' Guarnero yelled.

Rossini hit him on the head with the barrel of the Beretta. Not too hard, just hard enough to make him correct his manners. 'Either you tell us the whole story or we'll truss you up like a turkey and phone your colleagues here in Rome. Imagine how many questions they'll be wanting to ask when they find this dossier on Jacovone lying on the bed here on open display.'

The threat proved effective. 'It's a personal matter.'

'Let me guess. You were one of his favourite actors and he didn't pay you,' I said, needling him.

He bowed his head. 'It's my sister,' he whispered.

Marisa Guarnero, thirty years old, had posted an ad on an S&M website, offering her services as a slave. She had agreed to meet a master who had taken her to a hotel. The third time they met, he turned up with the blackmail video. Marisa taught Italian at a middle school, was unmarried and had a boyfriend working in Switzerland. She also had a brother in the police who was married with two children, a father who worked in a factory, and a mother who was a nurse. She had surrendered to the blackmail and had 'acted' in several videos. Then, when the blackmailers' demands had become too pressing, she had gone for a walk in a Turin park, sat on a bench, gulped down some rat poison and waited to die. Her brother, spurred on by his policeman's intuition, had decided to investigate. He couldn't understand why Marisa had killed herself without leaving any trace of an explanation. During his training it had been impressed upon him that suicides without suicide notes were always suspicious. Flicking through his sister's address book, he had come across a nickname: sorrisoblu. He had switched on her computer and gone online. When asked, 'Have you forgotten your password?', he clicked on 'Yes'. Then, once he'd typed in his sister's date of birth and address, the computer had given him the clue he needed. 'What is my cat's name?'

Guarnero had tapped in the name 'Arturo' and was appalled to discover that his sister had been leading a double life as a sexual deviant. Good thing she had topped herself – the family name and his career were safe. To make quite sure the secret was buried along with Marisa, Flavio had carefully sifted through his sister's computer files. Under 'My documents', he had discovered a sort of diary in which his sister related how she had been blackmailed and where she gave an account of everything she had suffered at the hands of a gang led by the Master of Knots. Flavio realized he'd been over-hasty in condemning her; the only thing

Marisa deserved was to be avenged. Logging on to the interior-ministry computer system, Flavio had searched for traces of the blackmailers but found nothing. He had then followed the porn-trafficking lead and eventually identified Jay Jacovone. Guarnero waited for his summer holidays, drove his wife and kids down to his in-laws in Calabria, and then headed back up to Rome.

'What were you planning to do?' I asked.

'Identify the gang.'

'And how were you going to do that?' Rossini asked. 'By tailing Jacovone in your mustard-coloured Fiat Punto?'

'What else do you know about Jacovone?' I enquired.

'Just what's contained in that report,' Guarnero replied.

Rossini removed the magazine and chucked the gun on the bed. 'Go back to your wife and kids and stay out of this mess,' Rossini advised him in a fatherly tone of voice. 'Focus on reaching retirement age without getting yourself killed.'

'We could really have done without that dickhead of a cop wasting our time,' Rossini fumed, as we walked back to the scooter.

'We gave him plenty of time to print our faces clearly in his memory.'

'He won't say a word; he has too much to lose.'

'Better not take any risks. It's time we headed back to Padova.'

'There's no rush,' Beniamino remarked, pulling on his helmet. 'My guess is that Guarnero knows a lot more than he's letting on.'

'You want to go on tailing him?'

'Yes, I do. I'm curious to see what he has in mind.'

Guarnero emerged from his hotel at about seven thirty and went into a rosticceria, where he listlessly consumed a pizza slice and an orangeade of a most improbable colour. Then he got back in his car and drove slowly, one eye riveted to his rear-view mirror, obviously afraid he was being followed. He went twice round the same roundabout in an effort to shake out anyone trying to tail him, but Rossini deftly avoided falling into that trap. The cop then led us to the San Saba district and parked his Punto in a position from which he could keep an eye on a modest little detached house. The area was almost deserted. Every now and then a car drove past, and of the few pedestrians about, most were walking their dogs.

About twenty minutes later, the street was suddenly lit up by the headlights of Jacovone's white Jaguar. It sped past the house, then turned up the first side street. Guarnero's Punto didn't make a move. A couple of minutes later, we noticed two people walking towards the house: one of them was Jacovone, the other was a short, thickset man. The short guy pulled out a set of keys and opened the armoured front door after disarming the intruder alarm, and the two men disappeared inside. Guarnero had done us a favour. He had led us straight to the headquarters of Jacovone's illegal porn-trafficking operation.

Rossini walked over to Guarnero's Fiat Punto.

'Out you get.'

Guarnero leapt out of his skin. He hadn't been expecting to see us there. He thought he was pretty smart but was really just an ordinary guy blinded by his lust for revenge. 'Get out of here,' he hissed, opening his car door.

'Otherwise you'll do what, call the police?' I said.

'Hand over the gun,' Beniamino ordered.

'No way.'

Rossini used his left hand to grab the cop by the throat and push him up against the car and his right one to relieve him of his handgun. He checked it was loaded, then tucked it into the top of his trousers, covering it with his shirt. 'Now, let's go and have a chat with our American friend.'

'You're both mad. Besides, it's not him I'm interested in. I want the Master of Knots.'

'And you hope to get to him by tailing this Mafioso? With your innate talent, a lifetime won't be long enough.'

Old Rossini climbed over the gate and jumped down into the garden while I dragged the cop over to the entryphone. I pressed the buzzer several times in quick succession.

'Who is it?' someone asked in a heavy Rome accent.

'Police.'

Nothing happened. After a few seconds we heard a noise like a door being kicked in. Then silence. Finally Beniamino opened the front door. As we stepped inside, I saw Jacovone and his associate lying on the floor, their hands clasped behind their heads.

'I caught them out back as they were trying to run away. This "godfather" here was even armed,' he said, displaying a short-barrelled thirty-eight-millimetre handgun.

'Who are you?' Jacovone barked in a tough-guy voice.

Rossini gave him a kick in the ribs. The Italian-American curled up in the foetal position. 'Fancy one too?' Rossini asked, glancing at Jacovone's sidekick. The short guy shook his head. 'We've come about the S and M videos,' Rossini went on. 'You are advised to cooperate.'

'If you're planning to steal them . . .' Jacovone began.

That earned him another kick in the ribs. 'Easy,' the little guy said. 'If you're not the police, we can come to some arrangement.'

'Give us the goods and we'll go,' I lied.

Jacovone and his sidekick led the three of us down to the cellar, through a heavy-duty bullet-proof door and into a room which, though not very spacious, was extremely neat and tidy. We used packing tape to tie Jacovone and the short guy to a couple of metal chairs. The video cassettes were lined up on some metal shelves alongside a security cupboard.

'What's inside?' Rossini asked.

Jacovone said nothing but his accomplice wasted no time. 'The master copies and some cash. Jay's got the key.'

I searched Jacovone and found his keys on his belt. The cupboard contained roughly thirty videos. I didn't count the money, I just stuffed everything into a sports bag I found under a table.

'That's all there is,' Jacovone said. 'So you can be on your way.'

I shook my head. 'First we need to have a little talk. We want to know who supplies you with this material.'

'I know nothing about that,' the short guy said eagerly. 'I'm just in charge of editing the videos and making the copies.'

'So you're the artist in this outfit,' I said.

'Jay's the one with the contacts.'

'If you know nothing, there's not a lot of point keeping you alive,' Beniamino remarked.

The little guy fell apart. 'Tell them, Jay! These guys are going to ice me.'

Rossini hit him on the nose with the gun barrel and the pain made him pass out. Rossini turned to Jacovone. 'Who is the Master of Knots?'

'Before I say anything, I want some guarantees.'

I burst out laughing. 'Look, we're not in America here. And, most of all, we're not the Feds. There's nothing to negotiate over. You talk or you die.'

At that moment we heard a stifled howl. Spinning round, I saw Flavio Guarnero looking at some photographs he had found in a drawer. I went over to him and recognized Helena, Antonina and Docile Woman. They were 'publicity' shots, taken from videos. Guarnero was ashen-faced and his eyes were bloodshot. He was clasping a photo, which I took from him. It showed a naked woman who had been tied up and was staring at the lens despairingly.

'Is that your sister?'

'Yes. It's Marisa,' Guarnero replied in a faint voice.

It was all over in a split second. Guarnero grabbed a pair of scissors from the table and lunged at Jacovone, stabbing him first in the chest and then in the throat. Old Rossini grabbed the cop by the shoulders and managed to pull him off the American, then slapped him a couple of times and tore the blood-streaked scissors from his hands. By this time, however, Jacovone's body was in spasm as blood gushed from his carotid artery and he was dead in under a minute. Beniamino and I took a good hard look at each other. It was entirely our fault: we had failed to take sufficient account of Guarnero's emotional state.

The cop now burst into tears. He was covered in blood from the crown of his head to the tips of his shoes. 'My God, what have I done?' he was starting to mumble.

Rossini gave him another hard slap. 'Shut it, dickhead.' He then approached Jacovone's accomplice. He placed the barrel of the gun to his heart. 'Are you sure you know nothing?' he asked calmly.

The little guy was too terrified to speak and just shook his head. Rossini pulled the trigger. The noise was ear-splitting. The man died at once. Rossini then pointed the Beretta into Guarnero's face.

'Don't,' I said.

'He's out of his head. If we let him go, he'll run off to his colleagues, spew out the whole story and we'll end up doing life.'

Guarnero looked lost and was babbling incomprehensibly. He had no idea of the danger he was in.

'Look. As soon as he's calmed down a bit he'll realize it's in his interests to keep quiet. He has a wife and children.'

Beniamino's arm seemed frozen. 'It's too dangerous. I can't take the risk.'

'Don't kill him. At least, not yet. Let me try talking to him.'

He shifted his focus from the sights of the Beretta and stared at me, then threw the safety catch and lowered the weapon. 'I'll give you ten minutes, just the time I need to build a bonfire to obliterate our fingerprints. If after that he's still not thinking straight I'll kill him.'

I shoved Guarnero out of the cellar and made him climb the stairs to the ground floor, then dragged him into a long-abandoned and filthy bathroom and pushed him into the tub. Rust-coloured water from the shower-head mixed with the blood washing off his face and clothes. He grabbed my arm. 'I've killed a man,' he whispered. 'I must tell my colleagues.'

'You're going to die if you keep talking crap,' I yelled. 'Think of your wife and kids. And your sister, while you're about it. If you tell anyone what happened here, the whole business with the videos will come out. You'll destroy yourself and your family.'

He started crying again. He was really pissing me off. Maybe a bullet in the head wasn't such a bad idea after all. I summoned all my energy for one last try, aiming the jet of water straight into his face and taking his breath away. 'Listen hard, Flavio,' I said, turning off the tap. 'What you do now is you go back to your hotel, pay the bill, join your family down in Calabria and keep your mouth shut about this.'

'I'm a police officer,' he murmured.

'You should have thought about that before coming to Rome. It's a little late now. In a couple of minutes, this building's going to burn and the cops are going to find nothing but two carbonized corpses.'

'Or maybe three,' a voice said at my back. Rossini was holding Guarnero's gun in his hand.

'Did you hear what the man said?' I asked Guarnero, shaking him by his shoulders. 'Are you going to come to your senses?'

'All right, all right, I won't say a thing.'

Beniamino walked up to him and placed the gun to his head. 'If you change your mind and land us in the shit, I swear to God I'll kill your wife and children.' He then removed the magazine and handed the gun back to its rightful owner. 'And just remember that your police-issue weapon has killed a man. The bullet's still in the body.'

I helped the man climb out of the tub and a puddle of dirty water formed at his feet. 'There's a nice fire smouldering away in the basement,' Rossini told us. 'We'd better get out of here.'

'Did you get their cellphones?' I asked.

'Shit. It didn't occur to me. Well, it's too late now.'

As soon as we arrived back at the flat, I undressed and went and took a shower. Beniamino knocked on the glass of the shower-cubicle and handed me a glass of Calvados. 'I don't kill women and children,' he said, seriously.

'I know you don't.'

'I just wanted to scare him, reinforce what you'd told him.'

'I know.'

'But it was still a mistake leaving him alive.'

'He'll not talk.'

'I don't think he will either, but it was still a mistake. Unprofessional, you know what I mean?'

'Yeah. But I don't give a shit.'

'You saved the life of a cop.'

'The life of a family man.'

He raised his glass of iced vodka. 'Here's health, then.'

Max the Memory was expecting us around lunchtime, but the Florence-Bologna section of the autostrada, where it crosses the Appenines, was congested with trucks and cars crammed with holidaymakers so I phoned to warn him we might arrive late. We listened to the radio news. Not much had remained of the two bodies in the cellar, given that Beniamino had built a pyre of videocassettes and laid the corpses on top. Plastic burned better than most things. The fire officers, however, were in no doubt as to the criminal origin of the fire. It made a brief item. As a story, it just didn't have the right ingredients to get worked up into that summer's real-crime thriller, the kind of thing you chatter about under the beach umbrella between a dip in the sea and an ice-cream.

Beniamino switched to a station playing 1960s Italian pop hits and we listened to Don Backy telling us a story all about a so-called easy girl, the 'ragazza facile' of the title. For the nth time, I took a look over my shoulder at the sports bag on the back seat. It contained the S&M video masters we had found in the security cupboard. And the money – something in the region of forty million Italian lire in banknotes of various denominations. It would help finance our hunt for the Master of Knots and his gang. If that poor idiot Guarnero hadn't carved up Jacovone, by this time we would have all the information we needed. Instead, we were back where we started. Old Rossini was hoping to find some helpful clues on the videos, but in my opinion it was a total waste of time. These guys were too smart to make any obvious mistakes.

Once we had passed the exit for the Bologna bypass, the traffic started to free up and Beniamino decked the accelerator. After a while he suddenly punched the steering-wheel and fired off some expletives.

'What's wrong with you?'

'That was a stupid fucking mistake I made, forgetting to take those bastards' cellphones. They could have been useful.'

'You're getting old.'

Rossini gave me a filthy look. 'It was just a joke,' I said hurriedly. 'In any case, I doubt if Jacovone would have used his cellphone to contact the Master of Knots. It was bound to be tapped.'

Max had prepared a cold meal: smoked ham, melon, pasta salad and, to follow, ice-cream. For once I really enjoyed my food.

'I went out the other evening with that woman I fancied,' Max said.

'The vegetarian?'

'Yeah.'

'And now you've gone off her?'

'Let's just say I have reservations. I don't like the way she laughs.'

'Then drop her,' Rossini advised in a fatherly manner. 'You can't just talk politics after you've had a fuck.'

After coffees, we moved into the study to watch the

videotapes, which turned out to be the unedited masters without any soundtrack. We began with the ones in which Helena had 'acted'. There were six in all. In the first one she was strapped to a table and gang-raped. All of her assailants wore masks but they clearly fitted the descriptions that Docile Woman had given us. In the other five videos, she was tied to a wooden structure hanging from the ceiling, and every now and then a masked and hooded man in a white tunic pulled on some ropes, thereby operating a system of pulleys. Helena looked like a string puppet. Each new position that Helena's body was made to assume corresponded to a new S&M fantasy and a different form of bondage. The terrified expression on Helena's face was very different from the look she had worn in the photograph Giraldi had shown us. Her mouth was held wide open by a rubber ball and her whole face was contracted in pain and terror. The hands of the man working the ropes moved with speed and assurance. He could be none other than the Master of Knots. In the final video, Helena was suspended in mid-air with her legs held wide apart and horizontal. It was as though she were sat dangling in space. The Master of Knots then approached her and took off his tunic. Unfortunately, he didn't make the mistake of removing his mask. We were, however, able to observe him more closely.

He looked about fifty. He wasn't tall but he was powerfully built, no doubt the result of assiduous weight-lifting in some gym. The tattoos covering his chest and back all depicted geisha girls tied up in a variety of ways – the kind of tattoos that Yakusas, Japanese mafiosi, generally go for. He had an erection. He penetrated Helena. Once he had withdrawn, he forced her to look at a rope flower, then he smeared his hand and forearm with a whitish cream. Helena had clearly understood what he was about to do and started to flail, but the ropes held her almost immobile. The Master of Knots then moved round behind her back. The camera followed him and we saw a close-up of his fingers as they insinuated their way in between her buttocks.

Max hit the remote and the picture vanished. 'I need a drink of something.'

'Me too.'

'That guy's a dead man,' Rossini announced. 'But it won't be a bullet that kills him.' He knocked back the corn vodka I'd brought him in a single gulp. 'Let's finish seeing this shite.'

Max's supposition had been right: Helena's death was a mistake. When he extracted his arm from her body, the Master of Knots was visibly annoyed with himself. Equally clearly, the deaths of Antonina Gattuso and Master Mariano were decided in advance. Giraldi was literally impaled, still conscious when the tip of the lance emerged from his shoulder. Antonina, after being savagely whipped and covered with boiling wax, was subjected to the same torture as Helena. The Master of Knots offered her a rope flower, too. According to Max, it resembled a carnation.

We watched the rest of the videos. There was one other that showed a woman with long black hair being fist-fucked to death – the Master of Knots clearly had a predilection for that particular torture technique. The other videos contained S&M porn performances extorted by blackmail. Apart from Docile Woman and Antonina, four other women were involved.

We remained for a long time in silence, drinking and smoking. It wasn't easy to say anything that made sense after what we'd witnessed. We'd never seen an S&M torture video before, let alone snuff. We were deeply shocked.

'What are we going to do about the families?' Max asked.

'What do you mean?'

'We can't make them spend the rest of their lives wondering what on earth happened to Helena, Antonina and Giraldi. It would be cruel.'

Rossini lit a cigarette. 'But we can't tell them the truth either.'

'It would be a nice gesture. But it's too dangerous.'

'Marco's right. Besides, the first priority is to hunt down those pieces of shit,' Rossini said. 'Everything else can wait.'

Max added some ice to his glass. 'I'll do a blow-up of the Master of Knots' tattoos. Maybe we'll get lucky and find the guy who does them.'

'Assuming they were done in Italy,' I added doubtfully.

'It's worth a try. Anyway, there's nothing else we can do except try to snare them with a website ad.'

'Let's hope Jacovone's death hasn't scared them off,' Beniamino said.

I rubbed my new Ronson lighter against my jeans to put a bit of a shine on it. 'I wouldn't worry. He had a lot of enemies. And for all the Master of Knots and his gang know, the job could have been done by one of his competitors or by some client unhappy with the goods.'

'Docile Woman told us that the Bang Gang doesn't do it solely for money,' Max reminded us. 'They're probably already on the lookout for fresh victims.'

'Let's start by seeing where the tattoos lead us,' Rossini suggested. 'We could go to Milan tomorrow and then on to Turin . . .'

'Well, personally, tomorrow I'm going to Genoa for the anti-G8 demonstration,' Max reminded us. 'I'll be away a couple of days, but I can get you a list of tattoo artists.' He switched on his computer and connected to the internet. It took him the best part of an hour to put together a list of names and addresses for every tattoo artist in Northern Italy.

Beniamino dropped his cigarettes, lighter and cellphone in his pocket. 'I'm going to take a boat trip,' he said. 'I need to spend some time on my own to get over that lousy video shit.'

Max stroked his prominent paunch. 'You said earlier you wouldn't be using a bullet to kill the Master of Knots. What did you mean?'

'I want him to be fully aware he's about to die,' Rossini replied seriously. 'Second after second after second of pain and lucidity.'

'Don't you think that's going a bit far?' I asked.

'No, I don't. But if the idea upsets your noble little hearts, I'll leave the matter in your hands.'

Fat Max and I exchanged a glance. We'd never have the guts to pull the trigger.

'Do as you like,' I said.

Rossini made for the door, then turned back and gave Max a pat on the cheek. 'Keep out of the cops' way,' he advised. 'And if there's any trouble, call us immediately.'

'I guess talking it over would be pointless,' I said.

'Right.'

I retired to my flat, wanting to be on my own to try drowning in alcohol the horrific pictures still stubbornly lingering in my mind. I started into the bottle without even turning on the stereo: there could be no blues sad enough.

Max knocked on my door in the middle of the night and followed me into the kitchen, where I gulped down a glass of iced water and a couple of headache tablets.

'Didn't you get drunk?' I asked.

He shook his head. 'I wanted to think.'

'And I bet you're now going to tell me in minute detail everything that's been rattling round in your head, right?' I mumbled, slurring my words. 'Ruining my therapeutic binge.'

'Those images made me think of torture; I mean the kind they use to make you talk.'

I sat down and lit a cigarette. Whatever Max had to say was going to take a while.

'I've been hearing about it for years now,' Max continued in a soft voice. 'When I was a kid the accounts of the Resistance, then later the stories that South American refugees told . . .'

'Make your point, Max. I want to get back to bed.'

'All those who withstood torture have become heroes, whereas those who surrendered have come to be regarded as traitors.'

I shrugged. 'That's the way life is. What's the problem?'

'While I was watching those videos, I realized I could never withstand torture.'

'I don't reckon I could either. Look, when I was arrested they beat me for an entire night. The only reason I didn't talk was because I knew fuck-all.'

'But Old Rossini never said a single word.'

'Like lots of others, including people you wouldn't bet a lira on. Maybe it depends on the situation you find yourself in.'

'I'm glad I was never put to the test and, anyway, I'm no longer so sure that those who talk under torture are traitors.'

'I don't know and really don't want to start worrying about it,' I snorted. 'The rule is that when you need information, first you ask nicely and then you break bones. Face it; it's a method we use too. Intimidation, violence and blackmail are the only techniques for making people talk.'

'Yeah, I know. It's just that I've never before imagined myself in a situation where I had to decide between talking and getting beaten to a pulp.'

'And there's no point in imagining it now, either.'

Max got up. He said goodnight with a wave of his hand and headed for the door.

'I've got a story for you,' I said.

'Another of your prison stories?' he asked sarcastically.

'Back in the days when grassing up your comrades was just getting to be the height of fashion, those involved in armed struggle began to lose any trust they had ever had in one another. So every time one of them went to see the doctor, the prison governor or the prison admin office, he had to be accompanied by a fellow comrade just to make sure he didn't cut a deal with the cops. But in the end they always found a way.'

'So?'

'Torture had fuck-all to do with it. The only thing they were afraid of was doing time and growing old behind bars. They got off lightly, every last one of them.'

'I can't see what you're driving at.'

'You can understand and forgive someone who talks because his nuts are in a vice. Anybody can have a moment's weakness, but ratting is something else. So before you get yourself into trouble it's best to work out whether or not you have the balls to do prison.'

'And you have?'

'Not any more. Whatever happens, I'm never going back inside.'

'Does Old Rossini see things the same way?'

'Sure. You play the game for as long as you can keep winning, then you let someone else have a go.'

'You bow out for ever?'

'It's the only way to avoid spending the rest of your life being fucked up the arse.'

'I understand.'

'Think about it, Max. Some things it's best to consider really carefully.'

Before leaving for Genoa, Max had printed out a dozen or so enlargements of the Master of Knots' tattoos. I took yet another long, hard look at them, then popped them into the glove compartment of Beniamino's Chrysler. We hit the autostrada at about nine a.m. The heat was still bearable and, anyway, the car's air-conditioning would give us adequate protection.

My associate was not in a good mood. I didn't mention the conversation I'd had with Max; he would only have made his usual snide remarks about the failings and feebleness of Max's and my generation.

'I've still got those videos lodged in my brain,' he suddenly burst out. 'Just think – last night I couldn't make love to Sylvie.'

'It happens.'

'That's what she said, too, and then pointed out that I'm not as young as I used to be.'

'And that's what really pissed you off.'

'You bet.'

'And so you had a row . . .'

'I got dressed and cleared off.'

'But you'll phone her this evening and make up.'

'By rights, she ought to phone me.'

'But you're a gentleman . . .'

'The thing is, I'm as love-sick as any teenager. I'd really like us to last a good while longer yet.'

'It looks to me like a pretty solid relationship.'

'But she's a nightclub performer. You know what they're like: one day they grow tired of wherever they are and just move on. And Sylvie's not so young either. Another few years and she'll have to retire.'

'Ever thought of marrying her?'

He burst out laughing and didn't reply. He turned on the radio. The news was all about the G8 Summit. Tens of thousands of demonstrators were converging on Genoa and the Minister of the Interior had stated in an interview, 'As long as I'm in charge, the Italian police will not open fire on demonstrators.'

Old Rossini knew Milan like the back of his hand, so we set about investigating the tattoo studios in a carefully worked-out order. By the middle of the afternoon, however, we were beginning to suspect that this was not going to lead us to the Master of Knots. In the evening, our fears were confirmed.

'Those tattoos were done in Japan,' Jack 'the Needle' Lovisetti told us. He was putting the finishing touches to a dragon he had been tattooing on a girl's shoulder. 'I'm sure of it. I've been to Japan and seen how they work. You can tell by the colours they've used and the way the designs are beaten. And the geishas have their genitals covered up, in line with Japanese figurative custom.'

'It could be somebody who learnt their technique in Japan.'

'Impossible – I'd have heard of them.'

'Is there no way you can help us?'

'No. All I can do is give you a nice tattoo.'

'No thanks,' I replied.

'I've got one I'd like improved,' Beniamino said enthusiastically. He removed his jacket and rolled his shirt-sleeve right up to his shoulder, displaying the image of a man and a woman making love under a palm tree in the moonlight.

'That's a really shitty piece of work,' Jack remarked. 'Where did you have it done? San Vittore prison?'

'Yes, as it happens,' Rossini replied dryly.

Suddenly Lovisetto no longer felt the urge to be funny. 'Well, there's nothing you can do about it. If you don't like it, your only option is minor surgery.'

I dragged Beniamino out of the studio before the situation degenerated.

'That guy ought to learn some manners,' Rossini scowled.

'Well, he does have a point,' I hit back. 'That tattoo really is ugly. And what he told us was helpful; we can stop wasting our time on this goose-chase.'

I tried to light a cigarette but my lighter was out of gas. Rossini reached for his 1970s Marseilles-Mafia-style solid-gold Dunhill. 'What you need to remember with lighters is every now and then to put in some gas.'

I took a drag. 'If we want to catch the Master of Knots, we'd better hope for a stroke of luck.'

'That bastard's not getting away with it.'

'Right now, he's got the upper hand.'

Before leaving Milan, Rossini wanted to stop for a pizza in the city centre. The restaurant proprietor pulled out all the stops. She had once been the woman of a bank robber who had done several jobs with Beniamino, and who had died in a gunfight with the Carabinieri as he was trying to make his getaway after raiding a bank near Brescia. The pizzas looked and smelled really inviting but I had eaten too many as a student and all I could now manage was a couple of bites. On the other hand, there was a Calvados sorbet on the dessert list, so I ordered one and washed it down with a glass of Morin.

Rossini asked the waiter if we could watch the news on the big-screen TV normally used only for following football matches. The G8 summit in Genoa was the first item. While the world's leaders had been pretending to work on a solution to the planet's problems, a massive protest march had moved off from Piazza Carignano. The pictures showed a sea of smiling people singing and dancing while thousands of police officers lining the streets observed them from behind the visors of their helmets. They were positioned to defend the so-called red zone, a section of the city that had been turned into a metal cage and declared off-limits to make quite sure the big shots weren't disturbed. There hadn't been a single incident. Reassured, I ordered another Calvados. I would have liked to call Max on his cellphone but I didn't want to act like a mother hen.

It was just past six in the afternoon and I was back home in my flat enjoying the air-conditioning and listening to some blues. Every now and then I drank a sip. Thinking about Virna made me thirsty. I was missing her. I was tempted to call her but couldn't think of a sufficiently casual-but-intelligent opening phrase. Then I heard some loud knocking at my door and through the spyhole saw a distorted image of Beniamino.

'Have you any news of Max?' he asked, sombre-faced.

I shook my head. 'Has something happened in Genoa?'

'An hour ago, the Carabinieri killed a demonstrator.'

I rushed to switch on the TV. Scenes of clashes. A body lying on the ground close to a Carabinieri jeep. White vest, jeans, and a blood-soaked dark-blue balaclava. A cop, realizing a TV camera was trained on him, started to yell at a masked youth who was running away. 'It was you who killed him, with that stone you threw, you piece of shit!'

I glanced at Rossini, whose arm swept the air in an angry gesture. 'It's all just crap.'

I turned down the volume and dialled Max's cellphone. He replied at the third ring. 'We're running for it,' he panted. 'I'll call you as soon as I'm safe.'

While waiting for Max to call back, we channel-hopped, watching the pictures from Genoa. I hit the mute – any commentary was superfluous. The demonstrators had fallen into the most classic of traps. Little groups of provocateurs and other morons referred to generically as the Black Bloc, backed up by a bunch of undercover cops, had had no trouble whatsoever in sparking the rioting, handing the police the excuse they needed to charge the march in a part of the city well away from the so-called Red Zone. Something of that nature had to have been planned in advance. There was a lot of new kit on display: shiny new American riot batons, a new form of tear gas manufactured in Italy under American licence, and flashy new body-armour that made the cops look like baddies in some old sci-fi flick. Then in the Piazza there were Carabinieri and riot police. The Guardia di Finanza officers were the most ferocious of the lot.

'From kickbacks to kicked heads: they're really making progress,' Rossini quipped.

Every now and then, the cameras trained their lenses back on Piazza Alimonda, where the demonstrator had died. By this time it had been established that he had been killed by a shot fired from inside the jeep and that the jeep had then run over him. In fact, the Carabinieri had opened fire several times that day, until someone ended up dead.

'He was just a boy,' I murmured. He was small and slender, his arms so skinny he had even managed to push an arm through a spool of adhesive tape that he must have found on the ground somewhere, and he'd worked it all the way up past his elbow.

'They're just kids,' Rossini burst out, beside himself with rage. 'And that goes for the white-haired old-timers too. They're just kids who've understood fuck-all and are still dreaming.'

My cellphone rang. It was Max. 'They charged at us without any warning when we were handing out Iraqi dates . . .'

'I couldn't give a fuck,' I yelled. 'Move your arse the hell out of Genoa.'

'No. I'm staying put,' Max replied calmly. 'I'm in an area now that's well away from the clashes. Nothing'll happen to me.'

'Don't you get it? We're not living in the 1970s any more . . .'

'See you, Marco. We'll talk tomorrow.'

I glanced at Rossini, then back at the TV screen. A police officer was firing a tear gas canister into a van full of injured demonstrators. 'He's not coming back,' I said. 'He has to finish handing out his Iraqi dates.'

Beniamino shrugged and lit himself a cigarette.

A few hours later, downstairs at La Cuccia, the air was heavy with tension. Maurizio Camardi got up on stage and put his sax case down on a chair. 'We've decided not to play tonight. We feel sad, indignant and worried.'

His words were met with applause, then we all raised a glass to the memory of the kid who had been killed, Carlo Giuliani. It was a miserable evening, charged with anger. A customer I knew approached my table. Twenty-five years earlier he had been a left-wing militant. 'If they'd organized the kind of stewarding service we used to have, the cops would never have dared lash out like that,' he said.

Old Rossini fumed. 'Another of your pathetic fucking lefty veterans.'

The customer switched tables and we resumed drinking and smoking in silence.

Then Virna walked in, out of breath. The tan she'd acquired down south suited her. I gave her a smile, thinking she might have come to see me. 'Where's Max?' she asked, sounding worried.

'In Genoa,' I replied indifferently, trying to hide my disappointment.

'I guessed as much.'

'He's fine,' Rossini interjected.

'Thank heavens,' she said, sitting down.

'What do you want to drink?' I asked.

'You've already forgotten what I drink?'

I ordered a glass of vintage Spanish brandy. Virna started talking about what was happening in Genoa.

'If you're going to talk about Genoa, you've got the wrong table,' I cut in.

She pushed her chair angrily to one side and stalked off.

'You really are a jerk,' Old Rossini said.

'Don't you start.'

'You resented the fact that she came here asking after Max.'

'I admit it,' I said. 'I was hoping she'd throw herself into my arms like the old days.'

Rossini shook his head, then looked at his watch. 'I'll see you tomorrow morning. If anything happens, call me, whatever the hour.'

I slept badly and woke up early. I made myself my usual cup

of instant coffee and switched on the TV, again turning down the sound. I didn't want to hear any bullshit. Beniamino arrived at midday. 'News of Max?'

'Nothing.'

'Call him.'

Max told me not to worry: three hundred thousand people had arrived in Genoa from all over Europe and, after what had happened the day before, the police forces would confine themselves to monitoring the situation.

'Horseshit,' Beniamino muttered.

The events of the previous day were faithfully repeated blow by blow. Undercover police and agents provocateurs were able to operate unchecked and the first police charge kicked off at around three in the afternoon. Tear-gas rounds were fired from helicopters and from police boats lining the coast.

The protest march was broken up into three sections and the demonstrators didn't know what to do or where to go. They held up their hands to signal surrender but the baton blows just kept on coming. No one was spared, not even cameramen, press photographers or paramedics with red-cross signs on their chests and backs. One high-up from the DIGOS – Italy's special-operations and anti-terrorist corps – who hadn't even bothered to put on a mask, was filmed kicking a fifteen-year-old boy full in the face while his men held the lad down. The cops used any quiet moments to have group photos taken of themselves in a variety of warlike poses. The streets of Genoa were streaked with blood and the hospitals crammed with casualties. The nurses hurriedly stitched them up before they were shipped out to the temporary detention centre at Bolzaneto, where they were placed in the care of men from GOM. This was a special unit of the prison police created for the purpose of quelling prison disturbances and 'managing' awkward or dangerous detainees.

The prisoners were forced to stand for hours facing the wall, their legs and arms spread wide apart. They were given fresh beatings and the women were threatened with rape by truncheon. Prison doctors in combat fatigues saw it as part of their job to go round ripping out earrings and body jewellery. The Justice Minister made a personal visit to the detention centre and subsequently declared he had seen nothing out of the ordinary. His statement astonished no one. He would do anything for his 'boys' and was the only government minister who genuinely believed that Italian prisons were luxury hotels: he had even complained to the press that cells were fitted with colour TVs. He had, however, omitted to say that the detainees were not able to switch channels and that, without the contact with the outside world that TV provided, his jails would quickly have turned into violent, rioting, hell-holes.

Hundreds of thousands of people were fleeing from Genoa. It seemed like it was all over but in fact, preparations for one final blood-letting were underway. Pretending they had been attacked, the cops burst into a school that the protest organizers, the Genoa Social Forum, were using as their headquarters – an authentic round of score-settling. The battered heads and broken noses were caught on TV cameras as those unable to walk were stretchered out. The TV showed a close-up of a policewoman in a black T-shirt emblazoned with the anti-capitalist slogan 'No Global!'. She even had a tattoo on her arm. But in her hand she gripped one of the new US-import batons. A handkerchief hid her face from view. Only her helmet was standard-issue: blue and shiny with the police coat of arms embossed in gold.

There was no news of Max; his cellphone appeared to be

switched off. By two in the morning, Beniamino and I were convinced he had been arrested, and I phoned Renato Bonotto, the lawyer. He was still awake, glued to the TV. He told me that in Genoa constitutional rights had been practically suspended and that lawyers were impotent. All one could do was wait.

At six a.m. my cellphone rang – a Genoa number.

'My name is Delia Manzi. Are you Marco?' the kindly voice of an elderly lady asked me.

'Yes, I'm Marco.'

'Look, my husband and I have found an injured man in our back yard. He asked us to call this number.'

'Let me talk to him.'

'My husband is giving him first aid in another room. Your friend is seriously injured and needs to go into hospital.'

'That would be dangerous, Signora. The police would arrest him.'

'That's just what he said. But you've got to understand that we can't assume responsibility . . .'

'Of course. If you could just hang on for a couple of hours, we'll come and pick him up.'

'We live in Corso Italia, but the neighbourhood is full of police.'

'Don't worry about that. What's the house number?'

When I'd hung up, Rossini took the cellphone and dialled the number of a Genoa nightclub. 'I want a word with Vagno.'

For twenty million lire, some people belonging to the Genoese Mafia agreed to pick up Max from his hiding place and take him to a services area on the Milan-Venice autostrada.

In the meantime I went and woke up Daniele Cusinato, a surgeon with a weakness for horse-racing who would happily treat anyone for ready cash, no questions asked. I accepted his price and told him to stand by.

Max arrived in the back of a furniture truck, stretched out on a mattress. He was rather pale, his head was bandaged, and one of his eyebrows was swollen and had a sticking-plaster on it. He gave us a smile but as soon as we lifted him he passed out from the pain. We put him in my car and headed for Padova.

'Go easy,' Rossini muttered. 'You want the speed cops to pull us over?'

'Max is in a bad way,' I snapped back. 'He needs a doctor.'

'Control your nerves, Marco. And don't exceed the speed limit.'

Max cleared his throat. 'Any more deaths?'

'No. But there are a lot of serious injuries,' Rossini replied.

'They beat me like a drum,' Max mumbled.

'How are you feeling?' I asked.

'Lousy. Never felt worse in my entire life.'

'Then don't waste any breath,' Beniamino said. 'We'll be at the doctor's before long.'

At the autostrada exit there was a roadblock manned by Carabinieri. As ever, my Skoda Felicia failed to attract their interest.

'It would be wiser to have him admitted to hospital,' the doctor told us.

'That's not an option.'

'He has concussion but I can't tell how severe it is,' the doctor replied gravely. 'There could be complications. Besides that, he has a broken left wrist, three broken ribs, bruises all over his body, and he'll need a dozen or so stitches in his head and a similar number in that eyebrow.'

'It's up to you, Max,' Old Rossini said.

'No hospitals,' he grunted. 'They'd arrest me straight away.'

'He could make up a believable story,' Cusinato suggested. 'After all, Genoa's a fair distance away.'

'The cops will be searching every hospital in Italy for people with his kind of injuries and bruising,' I said. 'Besides, his criminal record would blow wide open any story he could come up with.'

'Okay,' the doctor said, 'I'll do what I can to patch him up, but if his condition deteriorates I'll have to advise you to get him to the nearest A and E.'

Max waved his good arm. 'Hey, doctor,' he muttered, 'give me some kind of horse painkiller, will you? I can't take this much longer.'

I left the doctor's consulting room and phoned Rudy at the club. I told him to get us a van and something we could use as a stretcher. A few hours later we were easing Max down onto his own bed.

'Give me a cigarette, would you? I haven't had one since yesterday.'

I lit one and put it between his lips. 'So what happened?'

'I don't feel like talking about it.'

The doctor told us to keep you awake,' Rossini said. 'Besides, I'm really dying to hear what kind of fucked-up mess you got yourself into.'

'I was right in the middle of the march, with the rest of the people from the fair-trade movement,' Max started. 'All of a sudden these Black Bloc people appeared and started smashing shop windows, and then the police charged us. I ran but they caught up with me pretty quickly.'

'You don't have the physique for that kind of activity any more,' Beniamino scolded him.

'There were four of them,' Max continued. 'They kept kicking me and laying into me with their batons and it wasn't till I'd passed out that they went away. Then I dragged myself into the courtyard of a building and hid behind a car.'

'Which is where Signora Manzi and her husband found you, right?'

'Yeah, a nice old couple,' Max remarked. 'They called the caretaker and his son and had me moved into their house. I'm afraid I bled on their settee.'

'It's lucky nobody called an ambulance.'

'A lot of Genoese didn't appreciate the way the police were behaving.'

Rossini got to his feet. 'I'll go and order some flowers for Signora Manzi. It's the least we can do.'

Max wanted to watch TV. Almost every channel was still broadcasting pictures of the clashes in Genoa and interviews with leading politicians. The opposition was voicing concern and indignation, while the government was giving its full support to the actions of the forces of law and order. A journalist talked in a way that was subtly defamatory, about the young man who had been killed, while adopting a tone that oozed phoney sorrow for a young life cut brutally short. I turned down the volume.

'Turn it back up; I want to listen,' Max said.

'Aren't you tired of hearing crap?'

'Might as well get used to it. We're going to be hearing about Genoa for a long time to come.'

Someone knocked at the door. It was Virna. 'Rudy told me Max has been hurt.'

'Rudy talks too much.'

My ex-girlfriend ran to Max's bedside and showered him with kisses and caresses. It was at that point that I noticed I had some sleep to catch up on, so I left them to it. My flat stank of smoke so I threw open the windows and jumped under the shower. Knowing Virna was next door put me on edge. As always, I became awkward and tactless. For me to be jealous of Max was ridiculous, but I really didn't know what to do about it. I was still in love. I stretched out on the couch and fell fast asleep.

Over the next couple of weeks, Fat Max's condition improved considerably. Clearly he had a hard head. Cusinato came and examined him regularly and finally made up his mind to take him off the danger list. He was the kind of doctor who's very cautious with patients he can fleece. Virna was also often in attendance. She would prepare lunch and dinner and keep my associate merrily entertained. By this time I was openly avoiding her, but she appeared not to register my hostile attitude.

Max worried me. He was getting better quickly enough but his mood just got darker and darker. He watched TV and read the newspapers almost obsessively and was forever surfing the internet, checking out the anti-globalization movement's websites in search of news. Rossini noticed this too and was unable to control his tongue.

'You're really pissing me off, Max,' he said.

'Yeah? Why?'

'I can understand you licking your wounds, but you're coming on like a bloody martyr. It's unbearable.'

'Really?'

'Really. Besides, it's time we got back to work and focused on the Master of Knots. We've already wasted too much time.'

'Right now, I've got other stuff on my mind—'

Rossini leapt to his feet. 'I never wanted to get involved in this S and M crap in the first place; the two of you dragged me into it kicking and screaming. But I have no intention of letting go of it now. I swore a solemn oath I'd eliminate that sadist piece of shit.'

'Beniamino's right,' I said. 'The tattooing lead got us precisely nowhere. We need you to monitor the adverts at the S and M sites. It's the only lead we have left.'

Max lit a cigarette. 'You're both right,' he conceded with a sigh. 'I'm still pretty shaken. Not just because of the beating, but because of everything else that's happened. I can't think of anything else.'

'Well, it all seems crystal clear to me,' Rossini cut in. 'Just like it did even before it happened. They'd given you a pretty clear warning at the previous summit in Naples last March.'

'You're wrong about that,' Max hit back. 'What happened in Genoa has a totally different significance.'

Max would really have liked to go on thinking about it out loud, but our attitude made that impossible. It was a delicate moment – there was a real danger that a permanent rift might be created between us. Mediation was vital. Which, basically, is what I'm good at. I made a cautious proposal: we would hear Max out and then, once that was done, we would go after the Master of Knots again.

While Max talked, I realized why Beniamino had been so unwilling to engage in this discussion. He had grasped intuitively the kind of analogies Max might make with things in his past that he wished to forget. Whereas I, on the other hand, had just been surveying the overall situation from a distance without really thinking much about it, maybe because I was more concerned about what could happen to Max, and so I hadn't understood a thing. The way the cops had behaved seemed pretty normal to me and indeed, if we had been talking about prison or the use of violence against run-of-the-mill crooks and misfits, I'd have been right. But in Genoa the people on the receiving end had been peaceful citizens without police records.

In the 1970s, policing had been very different, the aim always being to contain street clashes. A couple of young people had lost their lives, but at least no open season had ever been declared on demonstrators, and there had certainly been no rampaging through hospitals. What's more, once those arrested had been handed over to the prison police the beatings had always ceased.

Genoa had been different. The women and men who had protested against the G8 summit were treated from start to finish like common criminals caught red-handed. In other words, the violence meted out on them was standard jail violence: the savage beatings of a single person lying on the ground, by a group of four or five officers, was the usual punitive 'Sant'Antonio' technique used in Italian prisons. The way the police burst into and smashed their way through the school used by the Genoa Social Forum as their headquarters was just how police would retake control of a rioting prison: an occupation force moves in, the rioters are beaten senseless and then immediately transferred to other institutions. And the special prison-police unit at the temporary detention centre at Bolzaneto had given their new guests just the kind of welcome normally reserved for dangerous prisoners arriving at a maximum security prison. As Fat Max spoke, analysing each detail of the way the forces of law and order had behaved, the TV images of the police charges flashed through my mind. The forest of raised hands, the terrorized faces and gaping mouths reminded me of something that had happened years earlier in the special prison at Cuneo. I closed my eyes. Just as I had done then when I felt the first truncheon strike my back.

Max had finished his piece. He poured himself another grappa and broke open a new pack of cigarettes.

'This is just a problem for you and your fellow-dreamers,' Rossini commented. 'We've always had to deal with these methods.'

Beniamino wasn't that wrong. 'I have to confess that none of this stuff surprises me too much either. Nor does it scandalize me, particularly.'

'It's a real morale booster talking to you two,' Max said.

'What do you expect?' Rossini asked. 'From where we're sitting, nothing's changed. And when I say "we" that includes you too. You're an outsider and a misfit and you always will be.'

'Nowadays even traffic cops lash out like wild beasts. They've forged papers and got their hands on guns and truncheons,' I said. 'Look at the way they treat the black immigrants who sell their bric-a-brac in the city centre under the arcades, and how they smash up street buskers' instruments.'

'You ought to be happy about it,' Rossini interrupted me, joking. 'At long last we have a democratic police force that treats everyone the same way.'

'Things are different now, and there's no going back,' I resumed. 'They'll use every means available to cut your legs away from under you, and they're not short of means: the mass media, the batons, the prisons . . .'

'And agents provocateurs,' Rossini added. 'These so-called New Red Brigades just stink of secret-service involvement. They'll use them against you to settle old scores. Just wait and see how long it takes them to round up the Italian political refugees in Paris and throw them into prison.'

Max smiled. 'Those guys are safe. They'll never touch them.'

'We'll see about that. "International Terrorism" can be used to justify anything.'

Max raised a hand to signal surrender. 'All right, you win,' he spluttered, connecting to the internet. 'Let's change the subject. How come you couldn't find out anything about the Master of Knots' tattoos?'

'Because they were most likely done in Japan rather than Italy,' I explained.

'A real shame,' Max muttered, shifting the mouse.

There wasn't much new on the S&M sites, and no great increase in the number of adverts since we'd last looked. Max said a bit of a lull was to be expected over the summer.

'We're well into the second week of August,' I pointed out. 'Almost everyone's away. Maybe the S and M gang is on holiday too.'

Max gave Beniamino a sly look. 'How come you're not at the seaside with Sylvie? The nightclubs are all closed right now.'

'Given the state you were in, I couldn't make any commitments. She was very understanding and went off to Spain with a friend of hers.'

Max burst out laughing. 'You're telling me that this year you'll be spending Ferragosto with the two of us?'

'Not if you keep up your wisecracks.'

But Max had turned serious. 'Take a look at this. There's a whole series of messages from Ivaz and Arakno,' he announced. 'Using their university intranet, they've discovered that Sherazade, the slave who was advertising for work as an S and M model has been contacted by a guy using the nickname Docktorramino, an anagram of Rock-Dominator, one of the nicknames on the list that Docile Woman gave us.'

'Ah, come on. There are hundreds of thousands of nicknames,' I said. 'Coincidences like that must be pretty common.'

'But not in an environment as restricted as the S and M scene,' Max replied. 'It was the k in docktor that made Arakno and Ivaz suspicious – it just looked like a deliberate error made to fit an anagram. But then, surprise surprise, the message is addressed to the only S and M model who has posted an advert since Helena.'

'I don't remember the ad,' Beniamino said.

Max reached for a sheet of paper and read out the contents.

I feel deep down I'm really a slave and dream of being dominated, but don't have any experience. I'm looking for expert masters willing to train me gradually in obedience. I'm afraid of physical pain even if I desire it, so for the time being I'm only making myself available as a model for photo shoots, during which I'm prepared to be tied up and penetrated. Write to Sherazade . . .

'Can we take a look at the guy's mail?' Rossini asked.

'Sure. Arakno and Ivaz have cracked his password.'

The inbox was empty. There was no new mail and nothing in the folders, just like the other email addresses the gang used. Sherazade's folders and inbox, on the other hand, were overflowing. A lot of her clients were previous clients of Helena. She had even received a couple of messages asking if she hadn't in fact just switched her nickname and email address. We examined all her correspondence and discovered she had already met two clients, the first in a hotel in Alessandria and the second in a hotel in Turin. She had charged a fee of two million lire up-front and had proceeded with caution, following all the safety guidelines. She had not yet replied to the email from Docktorramino, presumably because, as she had informed both him and a number of other potential clients, she was away on holiday and wouldn't be back till 17 August.

Max glanced at the calendar hanging on the wall behind him. 'Today's the twelfth.'

'We've got to hook her before they get to her. We need her as bait,' Rossini said.

'She answers her emails in the order in which they arrive so we'll have to wait our turn.'

'I've got an idea,' I said. 'Did you notice that neither of the two clients she met have sent her any more emails?'

'So?'

'I figure they no longer need to because she's given them her cellphone number.'

'Could be,' Max said, stroking his belly. 'Maybe she's a professional, just interested in building up a good client-base.'

'We could get the customers' details from the hotel records and find out their cellphone numbers that way.'

'And a couple of photographs,' I added. 'We'll need them to identify her by.'

Max pulled a face. 'We've already tried that trick and it didn't exactly work.'

'Because we were dealing with the Master of Knots' gang. These guys are presumably normal clients who would have used their true identities.'

Rossini looked at his watch. 'We could leave this evening

after dinner and get to Turin just in time to have a word with the night-porter.'

'We're going to have to leave you on your own,' I said to Max.

'Don't worry about it. I'm much better now and if I need anything I'll call Rudy. Or Virna . . .'

I gave him a poisonous look but he just smiled at me and winked. 'You can be such a jerk, Marco.'

'I know,' I said with a shrug. 'But I can't help it.'

In Turin we drew a blank. The night-porter turned out to be a retired Carabiniere officer. He only needed a glance at us to see we weren't looking for a room and when I showed him the money he picked up the phone and called the cops, forcing us to make an extremely hasty exit. Rossini ticked me off for failing to notice the Carabiniere Association badge the guy was wearing on his lapel. It was true; I had completely missed it. Bribery had become a habit. It was just so unusual for anyone to turn down money nowadays. Basically, furnishing information in exchange for a couple of crisp, fresh banknotes was really small-time.

We headed for Alessandria, a small town halfway between Turin and Genoa. I'd never been there before but at the end of the Seventies Beniamino had done a short stretch in the town's prison. We had trouble locating the hotel so late at night, but obtaining the information we wanted turned out to be easy. There was a student on reception using the night-shift to swot for his exams. From the title of the text book he laid face-down on the desk, we inferred he was studying for an exam in Criminal Law. The kid showed promise. He demanded an astronomical sum of money and we handed over a fistful of banknotes from Jacovone's stash.

The client who had rented the room was a man called

Romano Erba, born in Turin fifty-eight years earlier and currently living in Via Colombo, in the chic and central La Crocetta district of the city. We returned to the autostrada, drove till we came to a services area, then stopped and slept a few hours. At seven in the morning, a guy tapped on the car window.

'What do you want?' my associate asked.

'Zigarette,' the guy replied with a heavy foreign accent.

He must have been about forty, and his face was criss-crossed with deep lines, suggesting a life of rural poverty. He said he was Bulgarian. He stank of sweat and illegality. My associate gave him thirty thousand lire. 'Don't get caught,' he said.

'I could have slept another hour,' I muttered.

We went and had our first coffee of the day. It was going to be scorching hot yet again. A pig of a summer. I'd never liked hot weather and preferred the winter. I'd always preferred the winter. When I was at secondary school, if it was foggy when I stepped out into the street in the morning, I'd go straight to the station and catch a train to Venice. I loved to wander through the calli wrapped in a mass of dense white fleecy vapours. My associate also had a fondness for fog, but for less poetic reasons. It was the smuggler's best friend.

Beniamino bit into a croissant. 'I hope Max gets better quickly. He took one blow to the head too many.'

'I wouldn't worry too much.'

'He's burning up with anger and his type don't know how to handle it. They turn it all into politics and land themselves in the shit.'

'Max is too intelligent not to have grasped which way the wind is blowing.'

'That's not going to be enough to keep him out of trouble.'

When I rang Romano Erba's doorbell, the janitor came out of her cubicle and told me that Erba was on holiday with his family in Alassio, on the Ligurian coast. We could have guessed. Most Italians were away right now, either at the sea or in the mountains and the cities were half-empty. Turin was no exception. On the spur of the moment I came up with a tolerably credible story about some legal deed for the sale of an apartment requiring Erba's signature and the lady gave me the name of the hotel he was staying in. She said he had been taking his family to the same place every summer for years. Rossini groaned. He was tired of driving but there was still no way he was going to let me get behind the wheel of his smart new car; he said I drove like a pensioner. My view had always been that cars were necessary but dangerous. I would much rather use public transport, but in our line of work it was rarely practical. After Savona, the motorway snaked along the coast, with tunnel after tunnel. In one of the longest, we overtook a group of Dutch motorcyclists on Harley-Davidsons. The roar of the bikes was deafening. A girl waved to us.

Alassio was crawling with tourists. There was a row of English-style houses overlooking a strip of sand bristling with beach umbrellas. Erba's hotel was a four-star job patronized by people with money. A pretty blonde in a rather austere suit informed me that Signor Erba was having lunch.

'Tell him I'm waiting in the foyer.'

'Who shall I announce?' she enquired.

'Say I'm a friend of Sherazade.'

Within minutes, a worried-looking man was walking

towards me, glancing around. He was pudgy, medium-height, with a receding hairline and a pair of slender-framed glasses straddling an impressive nose. He was wearing a designer-initialled striped shirt and a pair of blue linen trousers.

'Who are you?' he asked, trying to display confidence. But there was nothing behind his aggressive manner except a terror of being unmasked or blackmailed.

'Doesn't matter who I am,' I said quietly. The blonde on the desk was watching us. 'I just want to know how to contact Sherazade.'

'I don't know her.'

'Would you like me to tell your wife that last month you met with an S and M model in a hotel in Alessandria?'

Erba went white. 'What do you want from me? Money?'

'Calm down. I already told you I want to meet Sherazade.'

'I don't understand,' he stammered. 'How come you know me? How did you know where I was?'

'That's none of your business. You tell me what I want to know and you'll never hear from me again.'

He wiped a hand across his forehead, undecided. I started walking towards the restaurant.

'Where are you going?'

'To have a chat with your lady wife.'

'Stop,' he said, taking a wallet from his hip pocket. He removed a business card from one of its compartments. 'Now leave me in peace,' he rasped.

'I could do with a photo of the model.'

'You've got to be joking. Do you really imagine I bring photos of her away with me on holiday?'

I looked him straight in the eye. He was lying. 'Yes, I do,'

I said. 'You're the kind of guy who keeps his photos close by, because without them you can't get it up,' I replied.

Romano Erba was doubtless unaccustomed to such uncouth manners but he was quick to realize that I wasn't about to drop the matter. He gestured for me to follow and we went down to the hotel garage. He pressed his remote key, unlocking a shiny white BMW, then, with trembling hands, he rummaged around in the glove compartment till he found the user's manual. Tucked between the pages were a couple of Polaroids. They showed a beautiful, shapely brunette with a wicked little smile, tied down on a bed. He handed them over with a grunt.

'Where does she live?'

'Turin.'

'Do you know the address?'

'No. I met her just once,' he replied, clearly exasperated.

'You can go back to your din-dins,' I said. 'And don't worry. You won't see me again.'

I stopped at reception and asked the blonde for the Turin phone book. I checked for the name on the business card. It wasn't listed. I hadn't expected it to be, but I still had to make sure. Sometimes you can get lucky.

I returned to the car feeling pretty pleased with myself and handed Rossini the photos and business card.

'Donatella Morganti, model and hostess,' he read out. 'It even gives her cellphone number.'

'A true professional,' I remarked.

'No doubt about that.' Rossini examined the pictures. 'Nice-looking, too.'

I dialled the number but got unobtainable. 'If she's on holiday like she told her clients, she'll be keeping it switched off to stop people pestering her.'

'You could well be right. All we can do now is wait for her to get back.'

'I've got an idea.'

'I'm listening.'

'You won't like it.'

'Then I don't want to know about it.'

'Remember Flavio Guarnero, the cop that killed Jacovone?'

'You're out of your mind.'

'Think about it. He works at police headquarters in Turin. He's got access to police computers. And if this lady's on the game, they'll have a file on her.'

'The man's mad. He can't be trusted.'

'Well, I reckon he can. If we tell him we need the information to get at the Master of Knots he'll help us.'

Old Rossini switched on the engine. 'Let's find a restaurant. I can't think straight on an empty stomach.'

It was an uphill struggle, but by the time the coffees came I had talked him round. All the way to Turin he assailed me with advice as well as his usual rant on how much things had changed since the old days. There was a time, he told me, when we would never have stooped so low as to ask a cop for help.

I called Max. He was getting better day by day and had now got his focus back on the case. I was tempted to ask after Virna, but decided against it, not wanting to make myself look ridiculous yet again. We reached Turin late afternoon. People were already trickling out of their homes, thronging the bars and cafés, knocking back iced aperitifs. Guarnero lived in the Barriera di Milano district in Corso Giulio Cesare. We found his block of flats and I tried calling him from a phone box. His wife told me he was still on duty but would be home in time for dinner.

We recognized his mustard-coloured Fiat Punto as soon as it turned into the road and by the time he got out of his car we were right behind him.

'Ciao, Flavio,' I said.

He spun round and his hand shot to the belt-holster where cops keep their guns in the summer, when they've no jacket to hide them.

Rossini spread his arms. 'I'm not armed.'

'What do you want?'

'We may have come up with something that could lead us to the Master of Knots, but we need your help.'

He shook his head. 'I don't want anything more to do with it.'

'And your sister?'

'I killed a man.'

'Jacovone was a piece of shit.'

'I'm leaving the force. I'm going to move down to Calabria. I've got a job lined up working with my father-in-law.'

I held the photo of Donatella under his nose. 'You're looking at the next victim. You want another person on your conscience?'

He knocked my hand away angrily. 'What would I have to do?'

'Check a name.'

'Is that it?'

'The name's Donatella Morganti. We think she's a professional who's moved into the S and M scene to broaden her customer base.'

'Okay. Call me tomorrow morning on this cellphone number.'

*

We grabbed a bite to eat then went straight to a hotel, as we were both tired and in need of sleep. As always, we found a place willing to give us a couple of rooms free of charge and not ask for ID – Old Rossini knew one such hotel in every town. I lay down on the bed with a glass of Calvados and my cigarettes within arm's reach. The TV was still carrying reports on the previous month's events in Genoa. The other side of the story, the victims' accounts, was now beginning to surface. There had been large numbers of film crews and cameras in circulation, and the thousands of photos and kilometres of film made it possible to reconstruct minute by minute precisely what had happened. Not that it changed anything. All those people earnestly mouthing words like justice and truth were going to achieve nothing for their pains. Nobody would be made to pay. Even the evidence would get buried under a mountain of bullshit. In the end, some expert would get wheeled out to support the most palatable version of events and forensic pathology would demonstrate that the young man had been killed by a bullet fired into the air that, as fate would have it, hit him on its way back down. A police association was up in arms about the use of a new type of tear gas with serious health risks; the cops, too, had inhaled a lot of the stuff. I switched to a shopping channel. There was nothing better for sending me to sleep.

I called Guarnero at eleven on the dot, using a public call box at the Porta Nuova train station in Turin. I didn't want any trace of our conversation hanging around on my cellphone. Guarnero informed me that the police had Donatella Morganti on file as a prostitute. They had hauled her in after a raid on an upmarket brothel that fronted as a beauty parlour and was used mainly by company executives and footballers. That was the last time she had been stopped. She lived in Via Cavour, in a flat that belonged to her father.

I wished him the very best of luck and put the phone down. Rossini glanced skywards. It had come naturally, spontaneously. If one disregarded the uniform he wore, Guarnero was an ordinary guy who had broken the rules of the world in which he lived in order to try and obtain some justice. And I was sure he would be hounded by remorse for the rest of his days.

We drove to Via Cavour, where Donatella lived on the third floor of a swanky apartment building. There was a sign saying that the janitor's lodge closed at six p.m. We made a note of that and returned to Padova.

Max's condition and general mood had continued to improve; he had started cooking again and listening to music. When we arrived, an old Beatles record was playing. Personally, I'd never much liked them. I grew up listening to Jefferson Airplane, Jimi Hendrix and the Rolling Stones, then one night I'd heard the voice of Janis Joplin and the Blues had gone straight to my heart. Max announced that his convalescence was over and that he was intending to accompany us to Turin to take part in our investigations.

'On one condition,' Rossini insisted. 'That you don't start breaking our balls all over again about prison and police beatings.'

Max beamed in amusement and unwrapped a milk chocolate. He was unlikely to stick to any such condition. Besides, there was no avoiding the issue. What had happened in Genoa was all people were talking about and the press and TV were busy stoking up a controversy.

For Ferragosto, Italy's August Bank Holiday, Beniamino took Max and me out on his motorboat. We were both as white as mozzarellas and had to smear dollops of sun-block all over our bodies. The sea was calm and we stopped for lunch at an expensive restaurant on the island of Torcello – a pleasant day spent among friends. Rossini told smuggling stories and Max recounted the first time he ever went camping in the mountains as a boy scout, while I kept quiet and listened. Whatever past I'd had before going to prison was well buried in some corner of my memory and I was in no mood to go digging around. The present was all that interested me.

The next day we left for Turin. Our plan was simple: we would wait for Donatella Morganti in her apartment. Rossini had brought with him his set of picklocks, as well as a handgun fitted with a silencer, concealed in a compartment that a car-body specialist he knew and trusted had created in the boot of his Chrysler.

We took turns to watch the street and the building where the woman lived. Quite a few of the apartments were empty, as a lot of people were still away on holiday. This could be either a good or a bad thing. On the one hand, there was less risk of attracting attention. But on the other, janitors were extra vigilant, on the lookout for summer-season cat-burglars.

We waited till mid-evening, then Beniamino used one of his picklocks on the block's main-entrance door. We slowly climbed the stairs to the third floor and found that the apartment adjacent to Donatella's was conveniently empty. Her door was fitted with a double lock. The security lock, worked by a butterfly-key was the main problem, and getting it open without damaging it took about twenty minutes. It was a good thing there were no alarms.

The apartment was in total darkness and stank of old air. We turned on our torches and quickly searched the place.

There was a living room, two bedrooms, one of which was used as a study, a bathroom and a kitchen. Max switched on the computer and started to go through the files. Rossini and I went into the kitchen and checked out the fridge. Apart from a couple of yogurts past their best-by dates and some packets of low-calorie cheese, there was nothing of any interest. Rossini found a bottle of wine, a tin of tuna and some crackers and improvised a snack. I kept him company, sipping from a bottle of Calvados I had had the foresight to bring along with me. I listened to the messages on the answering machine. There was one from her sister and one from her financial adviser – when it came to investments, Donatella knew exactly what she wanted. Next I took a look at her bedroom. She had good taste and enjoyed spending money on shoes and clothes; nothing flashy, not even in her underwear drawer. There wasn't anything in her entire wardrobe to connect her with her line of work. It just seemed like the home of a woman with a good job who had decided to live alone. On her bedside cabinet and chest of drawers, next to some bottles of perfume and a couple of cheap-edition romantic novels, there were several framed photos of her surrounded by her family. Donatella Morganti was evidently a very private person. The other tenants in the block were no doubt quite unaware of the fact that that good-looking young woman who lived on the third floor was a hooker enmeshed in S&M.

I lit a cigarette and stretched out on the bed. Max came into the room. 'There's absolutely nothing on that computer,' he whispered. 'She only uses it to go on the internet. Judging by her previous connections, she's a regular visitor to porn sites.'

I pointed my torch at the photographs. 'She's better-looking than I thought. Signor Erba's Polaroids don't do her justice.'

'She's on her own and wide open to blackmail: the perfect victim for the Master of Knots and his gang.'

'And we're not going to be very nice to her either.'

'We have no choice. Let's just hope that Arakno's and Ivaz's intuition is right.'

Hanging round in that flat, in the dark, without making a sound, was totally exasperating, especially in that heat. Luckily, Donatella Morganti arrived in the early afternoon of the following day.

We heard the key turn in the lock and the woman mutter in astonishment, 'Hell, the place reeks of smoke,' as she put her suitcase and bag on the floor. Switching on the light, she saw three strangers observing her with interest. She opened her mouth to let out a scream but Rossini's hand stopped it just in time.

'Shut it,' he whispered, waving the silenced gun at her.

Rossini forced her to sit down on an armchair and issued one of his classic threats before letting her speak. She really was a fine-looking woman. About thirty-five, tall, slim yet curvy in all the right places, and with long black shoulder-length hair worn loose she had an impertinent little face, large dark eyes and well-drawn lips. She was wearing a short, floral-pattern dress, which showed off her long, bronzed legs, and on her feet a pair of simple but elegant sandals. She wasn't wearing any showy jewellery, just a string of pearls round her neck, gold earrings, and a couple of rings on her fingers. In another situation, I mused, I might have hit on her. The thought only lasted a second; the moment she opened her mouth, I changed my mind.

'All I've got is a little money and not much jewellery,' she began in a shrill, unpleasant voice. 'If you just want to fuck me there's no need to hurt me.' This woman was tough all right. Despite the surprise and the fear she had to be feeling, she still managed to keep calm and look for the least-damaging way out.

Beniamino chuckled. 'Shit, she sounds just like the witch in *Snow White*.'

'We're not interested in robbing or raping you,' I told her. 'Quite the reverse. In fact, Sherazade, we're here to save your arse.'

The sound of the nickname she used as an S&M model undermined her confidence somewhat. 'Are you from the police?'

Max pulled up a chair and sat down facing her, then explained the danger she had been getting herself into and told her precisely what we wanted her to do.

'No way I'm doing that,' she squawked. 'I got into this scene to build up a clientele of wealthy older men. That's my target. They pay well for special services and that's all there is to it. If you think you can use me as bait to attract a bunch of dangerous perverts, you're out of your heads.'

'The way I see it, you have no option,' I said. 'Besides, nothing ever happens at a first meeting.'

'If you do not cooperate you are dead,' Rossini added slowly, separating the words out for the sake of clarity. It always fell to him to play the bad guy.

'Listen, you guys, there's nothing I can do to help you,' Donatella said, sounding reasonable. 'I'm new to this scene. I only got into it because business is slow right now in Turin for freelancers like me.'

Rossini raised his gun and pulled the trigger. The bullet lodged itself in the upholstery of Donatella's armchair, a couple of centimetres from her right ear. All we had heard was a brief click and then the tinkling sound of the bullet case as it hit the floor tiles. The room filled with the smell of cordite.

'The next one won't miss,' Beniamino muttered.

Donatella Morganti had turned as white as a marble tombstone. She threw her arms out wide. 'All right, put that thing away.'

Max nodded towards the study. 'Go to your computer and send this Docktorramino a message.'

Donatella wanted to obey but when she tried to stand up her legs folded beneath her and she fell back into the armchair. I went to the kitchen and got her a glass of water, which she drank straight down. I offered her a cigarette but she waved it away.

By this time Max had connected her computer to the internet. She took his place. 'What do I have to write?'

'Just that you want to meet him but that tomorrow is the only time you're free,' Max explained. 'And preferably not too far from Turin.'

Donatella tapped in the message. 'It won't work,' she muttered. 'There isn't enough time to organize a meeting.'

'In that case,' I snapped, 'you're going to have to put up with our company a while longer.' I was beginning to find her downright disagreeable.

We let her take a shower and go to the toilet but otherwise never let her out of our sight. To avoid any hassle, we ordered her to turn off her cellphone and not to answer her land-line. Max kept an eye on her inbox.

Docktorramino sent his reply just before midnight. He said he would very much like to meet her and suggested a luxury hotel in the centre of Turin not far from Porta Nuova station. He'd wait for her in the hotel bar at ten p.m. Then he gave her a cellphone number and asked her to ring the following morning to confirm.

'That's odd,' Max said. 'As far as we know, up to now the Bang Gang has only ever communicated by email.'

I screwed up the empty cigarette packet. 'Maybe they're in a hurry to put together another network of victims they can blackmail.'

'I reckon they find our bait's incautious haste a little suspicious,' Beniamino said. 'They want to make quite certain it's not a set-up.'

We debated the situation for another couple of minutes, till Donatella interrupted us. 'I'm hungry,' she said.

'The cupboard's empty.'

'I know. It's my flat.'

'Maybe there are some crackers left,' Max said.

'There's a pizzeria on the corner. It's open late.'

We looked at one another. I felt like stretching my legs. 'I'll go.'

'Better not,' Rossini said. 'Someone might notice you.'

'I could have them delivered,' Donatella suggested. 'It wouldn't be the first time – the manager has a soft spot for me.'

'You might be planning to play some dumb trick,' Old Rossini said.

'I'm hungry, that's all,' Donatella snapped.

'You've been warned.'

She dialled the pizzeria number from memory and a quarter of an hour later a delivery boy showed up with pizzas and cans of beer. She paid him at the door, preventing him from stepping over the threshold, while Rossini kept his weapon trained on her. We had a feast of a meal. Donatella relaxed and started chatting, telling us about the holiday she had just had on the island of Panarea off the coast of Sicily. She had been the guest of an ageing industrialist from the Le Marche region of Central Italy who had never got used to spending his holidays alone after the death of his wife. He liked to be seen with a good-looking brunette on his arm. They had been to bed once or twice but mostly they just talked. The job had netted her a million lire a day.

'Anyway, who are you guys?' she then asked point-blank.

None of us said a word. She had another go, running through a number of hypotheses, but after a while she gave up and went off to bed in a sulk.

She woke up around eight a.m, while I was on guard duty, made coffee and brought me a cup. I told her there was a message on her answering machine from her financial adviser. I only mentioned it out of idle curiosity but she was happy to tell me all about her plans. Donatella Morganti had the same dream as every other hooker: to stay on the game a few more years and invest her hard-earned money in some highly profitable business or other. I was tempted to say it was a dream that rarely came true, but refrained. It would have been a waste of breath. Besides, I didn't much care what happened to her.

A couple of hours later she rang the cellphone number that Docktorramino had given her. Beniamino had guessed right. He bombarded her with questions, trying to make quite sure she really was an S&M model. She answered skilfully – we had coached her on how to get him to believe what was in fact the truth, that she was a professional hooker. Docktorramino then probed carefully to see if she had a pimp, a worry she dispelled at once. Finally, she provided a description of herself and the clothes she would be wearing when they met.

When she put the phone down, Old Rossini took hold of her chin and forced her to look him in the eye. 'I won't be able to stay as close to you as I'd like this evening and you may feel tempted to sneak away. If you do, you're dead.'

She broke free, clearly furious, and said, 'Quit threatening me.'

'It's for your own good,' Rossini explained. 'This is the kind of business where mistakes just aren't allowed.'

A couple of hours before the rendezvous, Max and I took up position at a table in the hotel bar, wearing clothes and shoes we had bought that afternoon at a city-centre shop. Beniamino, as ever, had come supplied with a wardrobe suitable for all conceivable circumstances. Max and I looked like a pair of travelling salesmen. To slip more convincingly into my role, I'd even taken out my earring. It was time for dinner and the place was deserted. The barman fixed us a couple of vodka Martinis. Beniamino was going to bring Donatella to the hotel on the dot of ten p.m.

'I feel a little edgy,' Max said, filling his mouth with peanuts.

'Me too. Our plan's full of holes.'

'It was the best we could think up.'

'What if we lose the guy?'

'We'll have to force Donatella to meet him again.'

'That's just what I'm worried about.'

After nine, the bar got more lively: drinkers, hotel guests who didn't know what to do with their evening, and the odd business meeting. There were several men on their own but none of them looked anything like the descriptions Docile Woman had given us or the masked sadists we had seen for ourselves in the videos.

'I'll be going back to Genoa next year,' Max announced. 'The movement is going to converge there to mark the anniversary of the death of Carlo Giuliani.'

'Right. So the beating you took didn't teach you a thing.'

Max sipped at his third cocktail. I had switched to

Calvados. 'I've given some careful thought to what you and Old Rossini said, and I can't agree.'

'Yet it was one hundred per cent pure distilled wisdom,' I joked.

'You both assume things can never change, but that just isn't true. And, besides, the new rulers of the world are taking the whole of humankind to hell in a handcart, which is a good enough reason to try and stop them.'

'I seem to recall talk just like that back in the Seventies.'

Max gestured impatiently. 'At long last something new is happening and I don't want to be left on the sidelines. Do you see what I'm getting at?'

I gave him a wry grin. Max was burning up inside.

'I'm sick of living from hand to mouth,' he went on. 'I'd like a different life.'

'I don't know what to say to you. Personally, I wouldn't know how to live any differently.'

Max stared at me as he stroked his gut. 'Forgive me for busting your balls with all this stuff.'

'We're friends, Max,' I said, serious for once. Then I added, with a chuckle, 'Though right now you do remind me of Virna and all her crap about how I should sort myself out some other kind of life.'

Max burst out laughing and grabbed a handful of crisps. I was really fond of him but there was nothing I could do to help; I could scarcely make sense of my own life and had long since stopped worrying about it.

A couple of minutes before ten, a man in his thirties strode into the bar. He was tall, well-dressed, wore his blond hair tied in a pigtail, and had the kind of physique it takes a gym to shape. Max and I glanced at each other: this could be our man. He sat down on one of the stools at the bar and looked round. He exchanged a glance with another customer who gave him a barely perceptible nod to let him know things were fine. My stomach churned. We had found the Master of Knots' so-called Bang Gang. Max was sitting with his back to them and so hadn't noticed their greeting.

'There are two of them,' I murmured, indicating the other guy.

He had arrived about an hour earlier and had acted like a bored hotel guest. He was a little over fifty, tall and slim with short brown hair and a goatee covering a rather weak chin. I reckoned it was his job to hire the room and set up the hidden camcorder but that it was the other guy who would get to meet Sherazade. If something went wrong, he could always claim the woman had made the whole thing up or somebody had sneaked into the room while he was out. After all, they couldn't use false documents every time they checked in to a hotel. It might be necessary for a kidnapping – like when they snatched Helena – but otherwise it was a pointless additional risk. And they were hardly going to try to abduct Donatella from this place. It was far too busy.

When Donatella walked in, wearing an elegant short black dress with a plunging neckline, every man in the bar turned and stared. The blond guy waited a moment or two then got up and walked over to her with a smile. They shook hands and he pointed her to an out-of-the-way table. I dialled Rossini's cellphone – it was time he too made an appearance. Donatella and her client were chatting and drinking cognac. I had the impression he was asking her some more questions, so maybe he still didn't quite trust her. The other man kept glancing in Donatella's direction and, to judge by the smirk on his face, liked what he saw. He was no doubt convinced they had got themselves another stunning slave.

Rossini joined us, wearing a dark blue double-breasted suit. He held out his hand, apologized for being late and sat down at our table. While he babbled inanities for the benefit of the other drinkers, I pointed the two men out to him. A smile appeared on his face too, though for quite different reasons. He touched the bracelets he wore on his left wrist. He couldn't wait to add a couple more. Donatella and the blond guy got up and headed for the lifts. She was smiling, relaxed, a true professional. The older guy remained in his place. Our bait had agreed terms: a million lire for an hour's session. I started watching the clock impatiently.

The need to stay sitting in the bar had compelled us to put away a great deal of drink. Max had even demolished several bowlfuls of appetizers. I had limited myself to a few peanuts, but it was time to stop drinking. We needed to keep our wits about us so we could tail Blondy. We'd decided to forget about the other guy. He would probably be staying the night and if Blondy gave us the slip we would still be able to find him the following morning.

The hotel had two other exits: the one used by staff and tradesmen, and via the garage. Twenty minutes later, one of us was posted at each exit. As soon as we saw the guy coming, we were to call the others on their cellphones. Donatella was the first to leave, by the main door. She saw me and gave me a wink – it had been an easy trick. Then came Blondy. He set off in the direction of the station, crossed the road, then turned down a side street. I followed him, keeping Rossini on the line while he caught up with me in his car. I watched as our man climbed into a large 4×4 and for a moment I was afraid we were going to lose him. Rossini drew up beside me just as Blondy was pulling away and we were forced to leave Max in Turin. I called him and told him to wait for us at Donatella's apartment.

Blondy drove nice and slowly, clearly not expecting to be followed. He led us to Milan, parking outside a gym in the

Isola neighbourhood. At that time of night it should have been closed, but as soon as he pressed the bell someone opened the door.

'We've found their HQ,' Beniamino said. 'I wouldn't mind betting the whole gang is in there watching Donatella on video.'

'It's not a bad cover,' I remarked. 'I can see now why they're all in such great shape.'

'Between push-ups and pumping iron, they organize some blackmailing, a few murders, and their S and M porn video business.'

On the wall beneath the gym's signboard there was a glass-fronted cabinet containing photos illustrating the different activities the gym offered. Despite the fact that the street was deserted, we decided to get out of the car and take a look. Rossini was armed and if Blondy had seen and recognized us events would have spun out of control. Beniamino was twitching with impatience to settle matters.

I took from my pocket the Ronson lighter, which I'd finally got round to refilling, and lit a cigarette. It was an excuse to light up the cabinet. There was a notice informing the gym's patrons that it would remain closed till the first of September, after which their courses in all the latest gymnastic techniques would be starting up again. Courses were also available in one of the most ancient of martial arts, karate. The karate teacher, who had apparently studied in Japan, was called Bruno Chiarenza. There were quite a few snapshots showing him breaking piles of bricks, but there was one half-length portrait that let us get a much better look at him. He had a full, strong-willed face, icy blue eyes sunk in deep sockets beneath bushy eyebrows. He was wearing a kimono slightly open at the chest, revealing a glimpse of tattoo. The face of a geisha. Chiarenza was the

Master of Knots. Rossini grunted with satisfaction and we went back to the car to wait, curious to see him in the flesh.

Instead, it was only Blondy and the puny guy Docile Woman had identified as the gang's cameraman. It was the cameraman we decided to tail, as Rossini was convinced he would prove the weak link in the Bang Gang's whole operation. He climbed into a Ford Fiesta and headed for the ringroad.

'What are you planning to do?' I asked Rossini.

'If he lives some place quiet, I'd like to invite him to take a ride with us.'

'You think that's a good idea? We know where to find them.'

'Precisely. He can fill in the last details for us.'

'I'm not convinced it's the right move.'

'It's time to wrap this thing up.'

The Fiesta stopped at the gate of an old house out in the country, not far from Lodi. We'd driven the last few miles with our headlights switched off, so he didn't realize he had been followed till he felt Rossini's gun at his neck. Rossini forced him into the back of our car while I got behind the wheel.

'Who are you?' he asked, terrified.

Beniamino punched him in the stomach. 'Shut it, dick-head.'

I turned down a dirt road. After a while, Rossini signalled to me to pull up. He opened his door and dragged the cameraman out by his hair, then made him kneel and put the gun to the nape of his neck.

'What's your name?' I asked him, looking round. We were surrounded by vast fields of soya. Nobody was going to disturb us.

'Ugo Giachino,' he said faintly.

'What job do you do?'

'I work for a commercial TV channel.'

'And, in your spare time, you make S and M flicks, right?' Beniamino asked.

'That's not true.'

Rossini fitted the silencer then shot the guy in the foot. He screamed and collapsed on the ground.

'If right now you don't open that fucking mouth of yours I'm going to fill your legs as full of holes as a pasta strainer.'

We smoked a cigarette, giving him time to pull himself together. He whimpered softly as he tried to plug the bleeding with his fingers.

'I've got two kids,' he blubbed. 'Don't kill me.'

'It all depends on what you tell us,' Beniamino lied. 'If it interests us, we'll let you go back to your brats.'

It was Bruno Chiarenza who three years previously had had the idea of putting together a gang. He had been an S & M master for a long time, ever since his first trip to Japan, when he had become aware of – and given vent to – his sexual inclinations. Using his strong personality and charisma, he had gathered a group of four loyal initiates, carefully selected from among the members of the gym. All of them viewed their karate instructor as a true spiritual guide. To dominate women and use them as slaves for their pleasure was the central purpose of all their lives. Their names were Graziano D'Introna, Franco Rocchi, Raimondo Fiorati and Michele Narsi. It was Narsi who had asked Ugo to join the gang as cameraman – the two of them had got to know one another through S&M websites. The Master of Knots had decided to move into the illegal porn video business so they had needed a professional. Giachino swore on the heads of his children he had never laid a finger on a slave. He was only interested in watching, and got excited looking through a camera lens. There was also a lot of money in it.

To begin with they had sold the tapes only to a limited circle of masters. Then Jay Jacovone, a Miami Mafia boss, had got involved, shifting the gang up a gear. Jacovone demanded images of fist-fucking and snuff footage, since that kind of material fetched a lot of money in the States and Canada. The Master of Knots gave him what he wanted. The women they blackmailed never rebelled, too terrified that the double lives they were leading might be made public. The gang had first made contact with Jacovone through Adelmo Pietronero, a Rome-based master who had ended up in jail in the States on porn-trafficking charges.

'Maybe that was the guy we whacked along with Jacovone,' Rossini interjected.

'So that was you?' Ugo exclaimed. 'The Master thought it was Jay's family that did him.'

'Why?'

'He said Jacovone had fucked things up for them in Miami and they'd never forgiven him.'

'So who are you selling the tapes to now?'

'Nobody. It's all stopped.'

'In that case, how come you're on the lookout for fresh meat?'

'The Master wants some new slaves.'

'Tell us about Helena.'

'You know a lot already.'

'You have no idea how much.'

'It was her husband who handed her over to us. Chiarenza wanted her to be in just the right psychological situation so he could fist-fuck her.'

'Did Giraldi know his wife was going to be kidnapped?'

'Sure. The Master was blackmailing him too but, in any

case, he got off on the idea of Helena being dominated by other guys.'

'And afterwards you killed him along with Barbie Slave, right?'

'That was decided at the outset. It just sped things up a bit when Helena accidentally got killed.'

'Where's the tape you made this evening?'

'At the gym.'

'Did you enjoy it?'

Giachino didn't answer.

'It's getting late,' Beniamino said. 'You got any more questions for this piece of shit?'

'Just the addresses of his accomplices.'

Giachino reeled them off one after another, then he gave us an important piece of news. 'The Master is off to Japan in a week's time.'

'Well, thanks for the information,' I said.

'Let me get to a hospital, will you?'

'Wait a minute: first I want to sing you a little ditty,' Rossini said.

'Wh-what?' Giachino stammered.

'Just one little verse. You'll see, you'll like it:

> ' "The King of Marabella
> Liked to dance the Tarantella
> But we, far wiser by half,
> Just had to laugh." '

'What the fuck does that mean?' Giachino asked.

'You really didn't get it?'

'No.'

'Doesn't matter,' Rossini said, pulling the trigger.

166

We drove back to Turin and picked up Max from outside Donatella Morganti's apartment block. 'Boy, what a pain in the arse that woman is,' Max scowled as soon as he had got in the car. 'All she could do was keep asking me when I was going to leave.'

'What did she tell you about how her trick went?' I enquired.

'The guy had some fun tying her up and then fucked her. Did you manage to tail the fair-haired guy?'

I told Max what had happened after we had left him in Turin.

'You shouldn't have been so hasty,' Max grumbled. 'This guy's death is sure to alarm the gang.'

I agreed with Max and had been repeating the same point ad nauseam to Beniamino ever since we had left Lodi.

'For now the main thing is to get our hands on the Master of Knots,' Rossini retorted. 'We know who all the other gang members are and I can deal with them in due course.'

'If Chiarenza brings his departure forward, we're fucked.'

'Well, we couldn't have known he was about to leave the country,' Rossini said defensively.

'Why don't you just admit you couldn't wait to kill somebody?'

Rossini gave me a filthy look and I told him to go to hell.

'Why don't we go and drop in on Chiarenza right now?' Max suggested. 'The body won't have been found yet.'

'I got rid of the gun,' Beniamino explained. 'I couldn't be wandering around with a gun I'd just used in a killing. Besides, I fancy something a little more powerful to deal with the Master of Knots.'

'What do you mean?'

'That guy's a black belt, and I'm not a kid any more. I

want to be using a weapon that doesn't force me to come in too close and that blows the guy away at the first shot.'

'You've seen too many Bruce Lee films,' Max teased.

'Do you remember that Dutch guy?' Rossini asked me.

I hadn't thought about him for years, or about any of the other guys I had met behind bars. He had landed in jail after killing his wife on holiday in Italy. Like Chiarenza, he was a martial-arts expert. One day he had had an argument with a Carabiniere officer attached to the jail. The cop had returned with a whole team behind him and the Dutch guy had beaten the shit out of every one of them, and then coolly returned to his cell. To get him out of there they had had to use tear gas, after which they gave him the full Sant'-Antonio: four or five of them beat him with batons as he lay on the ground with a blanket over his head. It put him in hospital for an entire month.

The sun was high in the sky by the time we got to Padova. Rossini left for home, saying he would be back that afternoon. He was going to get the 'tools' he needed and grab some sleep.

By seven that evening he still hadn't shown up. I was worried so I phoned Sylvie and she told me they had arrested him as soon as he arrived home. It turned out they had been waiting for him since five in the morning. For several minutes I couldn't move a muscle. I was devastated. Beniamino was like a brother to me and knowing he was in the hands of the police plunged me into the deepest despair. I held the cigarette lighter he had given me in my hand and squeezed hard. With tears welling in my eyes I went and knocked on Max's door.

'They've arrested Old Rossini.'

Max also took it badly and it was a while before he could

speak. 'There's no way they can have connected him to the shooting of Ugo Giachino,' he said after a long silence.

I threw myself on the couch. 'Give me a drink, will you?'

'Now's not the time,' Max said angrily. 'We need to speak to his lawyer and find out what he's been charged with.'

'I'd rather not. I don't trust the man. After his old lawyer retired, Beniamino engaged a slick young go-getter.'

'You mean the kind that's all politics, willing to defend anyone if the price is right, and always alleging communist manipulation every time a magistrate tries to raise the lid on the rich and powerful?'

'You got it.'

'I wouldn't have expected an old gangster like Rossini to hire that kind of lawyer.'

'Lawyers of the old school play far too clean to actually win trials and Rossini, given his criminal record, can't afford to take chances.'

'Then we're going to have contact Bonotto.'

I phoned Bonotto and arranged to meet him in a bar in the centre of Padova. We found him sitting on a stool with a glass of Negroni in his hand. He was talking with a couple of other customers and we had to hang around till they'd left.

'A colleague of mine in Venice told me that Rossini has been charged with holding up a security van in Mestre last night,' Bonotto explained. 'The investigators have no evidence whatsoever, just Rossini's previous convictions, but the fact is your friend hasn't got an alibi and so naturally they feel entitled to hold on to him.'

I was his alibi. Yet I could hardly go to the cops and declare that at the time in question we were in the middle of a field not far from Lodi bumping off a guy called Ugo Giachino.

'Is there any chance of getting him released any time soon?' Max asked.

'When it comes to legal procedures, soon is a fuzzy concept,' Bonotto said philosophically. 'According to his defence lawyer, there is every reason to be optimistic about the eventual outcome and, when you've got a criminal record as long as your friend's, that's the main thing.'

I felt like going round to Sylvie's to try and cheer her up, but Old Rossini's entire entourage had no doubt been placed under surveillance. Besides, I wouldn't have known what to say to her. I felt so despondent I was finding it hard to keep focused. I wanted a drink. I needed a drink. But it wasn't the right moment yet. Fat Max was reacting better than I was. We watched a couple of reports about the hold-up on the regional news. The security van, carrying cash bound for banks up and down the coast, had been held up by five gunmen at a junction on the Mestre bypass. They had used the well-worn trick of closing the carriageway with a truck jack-knifed right across it, then they'd fired off a few Kalashnikov rounds at the van to persuade the guards to open the doors. It was a sizable haul and the cops had promised to find the perpetrators fast.

'What are we going to do about the Master of Knots?' Max suddenly asked.

'I haven't the faintest goddamn idea,' I replied. It was the last thing I wanted to think about.

'We'll lose him for good if we hang around till Beniamino gets out.'

'Not necessarily,' I replied. 'He'll come back from Japan sooner or later.'

Max looked me straight in the eye. 'Do you really think he's that stupid?' he shouted. 'By now he'll know that

Giachino has been killed and he's sure to realize that somebody will have got him to spill the beans on the whole gang.'

'Without Rossini, our hands are tied. You surely can't imagine that the two of us could take him on.'

'Yeah, I reckon we could handle it.'

I burst into nervous laughter. 'The heat has melted your fucking brains. Neither of us has ever even held a gun.'

'So? It can't be that hard to pull a trigger.'

'Cut out the bullshit, Max. We've had some rotten luck and now we have to pull back a bit.'

Max stormed out, slamming the door.

'Go fuck yourself,' I yelled after him.

Rossini's arrest had unhinged Max, too. The truth was that without the old gangster's help we weren't up to tackling any really awkward investigative work. At most a case of marital infidelity or a hunt for runaway kids. Luckily, I had invested in La Cuccia at the right moment. But all I cared about right now was what was going to happen to Beniamino. When Max had gone to prison, I had really had a bad time. Someone dear to you behind bars is like a dead person who doesn't come back to life till they're released. I had no intention whatever of going through that again. Besides, I knew Old Rossini had sworn not to serve any more time, just as I had. No more prison. At any cost. I started shedding tears of rage and only alcohol calmed me down.

The following morning I went to see Bonotto and asked him to phone his colleague in Venice again. He did so straight away. From Bonotto's side of the conversation, I gathered that the police had found traces of gunpowder on Rossini's clothes.

'Things are getting complicated,' the lawyer remarked.

'He was with me the other night,' I said. 'Somewhere a long way from the scene of the hold-up. He used a weapon . . . just to check it was working.'

'Of course,' Bonotto said neutrally. 'And was the weapon he used of a different kind from that used by the security-van gang?'

'Beniamino used a handgun.'

'Well, in that case one can request a further investigation to demonstrate that the traces of powder found on his clothing are not compatible with the gun cases discovered near the security van.'

'Will it be enough to get him out of trouble?'

'Providing it can also be shown that he was elsewhere at the time.'

'So he needs an alibi.'

'Yes. One good enough to stand detailed scrutiny.'

Beniamino got news to us from his isolation cell by way of a bent prison officer at Venice jail. He was quite sure he would soon be released and he wanted us to organize a convincing 'performance'. While the cops had been busy trying to break his stubborn silence, he had been working on his alibi. There were a couple of Croatian policemen whom he paid handsomely to avoid any problems when he moored his boat in a particular harbour on the Dalmatian coast and who would certainly be prepared to testify that on the night in question he was with them, and that at the end of a long drinking session they had let him use their police-issue handguns to fire off a couple of rounds. There was no way the investigators would believe the story but they wouldn't be able to disprove it either. Rossini was too smart for them. I felt ashamed I had given in to despair. Instead of snivelling I should have realized Rossini would be busy organizing a winning move. Max was still in a sulk with me but we had other stuff to think about right now, so declared a truce.

One of the smugglers who worked for Rossini set sail for Croatia. Rossini's defence lawyer had been told by Sylvie that he would shortly be receiving some important information beneficial to his client's case, and now all they had to do was wait while the wheels of the law slowly turned. As a matter of curiosity, I went looking for information as to who had actually held up the security van. It only took me a couple of hours to discover that the job had been done by a gang of veteran Bosnians based in Udine. The cops also knew it had been done by non-Italians. In the heat of the moment the Bosnians had been overheard to exchange some words in their own language, but the police still stubbornly insisted on accusing Beniamino of being, if nothing else, the brains behind the robbery.

In the meantime I had continued to follow press reports relating to the murder of Ugo Giachino. He was described as an exemplary husband and father. Colleagues at the private TV station where he had worked pitched in to support his family and it was leaked that the Carabinieri HQ in Lodi was working on the theory that Giachino had been set upon by a bunch of Albanian thieves. In other words, the investigators were stumbling around in the dark. They knew perfectly well that nothing had been taken from Giachino.

In the middle of the night, Fat Max knocked on my door. In his hand he had the S&M videos we had found at Jacovone's hideout in Rome.

'What are we going to do with these?' Max added.

'C'mon. This is just an excuse to drag the issue up again.'

'You're right.'

'I don't want an argument.'

'The Master of Knots is due to leave for Japan in three days.'

'I know.'

'So let's talk about it.'

I sighed and told him to make himself comfortable. Max wanted to go back over the case from start to finish, in the finest detail. I took the view that it was a total waste of time but if it could help to convince him to drop his plans for all-out war I was only too happy to humour him. As I listened, however, I began to see things his way.

As he went back over the recent events I began to see the possibility of reopening our pursuit of the Master of Knots. There were a couple of problems: first, we would have to involve two people, neither of whom wanted anything further to do with us; second, the endgame was morally questionable.

'Beniamino will never talk to us again.'

'But it could work, right?'

'It all depends on Guarnero and Donatella.'

'Guarnero is wide open to blackmail and Donatella's in love with money.'

To persuade Flavio Guarnero to talk to us I had to threaten to spill the beans to his wife. He met us in a bar near the Turin police headquarters.

'Who's this?' he asked, pointing at Max.

'He works with me,' I replied.

'I've only got a few minutes. Got to get back to the office.'

'We've tracked down the Master of Knots,' I told him, showing him a photograph Fat Max had downloaded from the internet.

His ears pricked up and he listened carefully to the account we gave him. We omitted a couple of details, such as the death of Giachino.

'And what more do you want from me?'

Fat Max explained the plan. The cop stroked his chin thoughtfully, then knocked back his drink and, sticking the photo of Chiarenza in his pocket, said, 'Okay. I'll do it.'

*

'Not you two again!' Donatella Morganti burst out. She had just returned from the hairdresser's and I noticed her nail-varnish was a different colour too.

'We've come to offer you an excellent deal,' I said with a knowing smile. 'Plenty of beautiful cash and you won't even have to spread your thighs.'

'What's the catch?'

'Why don't you invite us in so we can talk it through nicely?'

The armchair Beniamino had shot a hole through had been replaced by a new one upholstered in red leather. Donatella crossed her legs. 'I'm listening.'

Once again it fell to Max to set out our plan, and Donatella interrupted him several times to ask for explanations. 'How much were you thinking of paying me?'

'Twenty million.'

'I want forty.'

'That's too much.'

'Then ask someone else.'

'Thirty.'

'Forty,' she hit back.

'All right.'

'Up front.'

'Twenty now and twenty when the job's done,' I said, handing her the envelope.

She felt the weight of it in her hands and stared me in the eye. 'You'd already decided on the price, right?'

'We thought you'd like to haggle a little.'

'You really are a pair of shitheads.'

Guarnero told us to meet him in a supermarket car park not far from his flat. He was looking weary and his T-shirt was stained with sweat. 'Chiarenza is catching a flight tomorrow morning out of Malpensa airport,' he said, handing me a piece of paper with the flight time and number. 'He tried to book onto an earlier plane but there were no available seats.'

'What else did you find out?'

He shrugged. 'Not a lot. He has no police record. He started a career in the parachute regiment, but left the service so he could devote himself to karate.'

'Married?'

'Divorced. No children.'

'And the others?'

'Graziano D'Introna is the only one with previous convictions; he was put away for indecent assault. The others are as pure as lilies. Each has a family, children, a good job.'

We had nothing else to say. After a moment's silence, he turned on his heels and walked away.

We picked up Donatella at her apartment and set off for Milan. She criticized my Skoda, saying she had never had a client as shabby as Max and me. She never stopped talking for a second and demanded we stopped and ate at a fashionable and pricey restaurant. The only way to shut her up was to go back over the plan. We found rooms for the night at a hotel in Saronno, not far from the airport, letting her have the only room with air-conditioning so as to avoid further whining. Max and I put up with sharing a hot, smelly, double room situated on the ground floor next to the kitchens.

Fat Max took a miniature bottle of spirits from the minibar. 'I wonder how Old Rossini is doing,' he said sadly.

I lit a cigarette. 'Right now he'll be stretched out on his cell-bed staring at the ceiling like every other prisoner.'

'Night's the worst time. I remember . . .'

'Don't, Max,' I butted in. 'I don't want to talk about prison. In fact, I don't want to talk at all.'

'You worried about tomorrow?'

'That too. Even if everything goes well, it's still the wrong ending.'

'It's all we can do.'

Donatella Morganti made her entrance at the airport dressed like a high-class hooker on a business trip. She had put her hair up and was wearing an elegant dark-blue suit. A crocodile-skin bag hung from her shoulder and in her left hand she was gripping a small holdall while her right hand pulled a little trolley along behind her. She made straight for the escalator. Then, after hanging round the boutiques for a bit, she went into a bar and ordered a cappuccino.

Max and I had taken up position near the information desks of the airline on which the Master of Knots had booked a seat to Japan. He arrived a few minutes after we did, with a lot of time to spare before take-off – he clearly didn't want to risk missing his plane. He carried a large suitcase in each hand without the slightest effort, and wore a pair of plain-weave trousers and a polo shirt that emphasized his massive pecs. He got in line at the check-in. Max alerted Donatella, who appeared almost at once and went and stood behind him. She tapped him on the shoulder and asked for some information. He turned round and the look on his face was pure amazement, though he quickly concealed it. Chiarenza had recognized her at once. He glanced round instinctively, trying to gauge just how much of a coincidence it was, running into the slave from the Turin hotel video like that. What he saw must have reassured him because he started chatting to the woman, seeming perfectly relaxed. He smiled a lot, displaying white, neatly spaced teeth. After a while, Donatella thanked him and walked off, pursued by his gaze. According to our plan, she'd have used the brief conversation to tell Chiarenza that her flight was delayed and she would be forced to while away the time sitting in a bar. All on her own, unfortunately.

The Master of Knots handed over his baggage and completed the formalities, then checked his watch. There was over an hour till boarding. He walked off in the direction Donatella had taken, caught up with her at a bar and asked if he could join her at her table. She gave him a big smile and pointed at the chair opposite, then immediately started hitting on him, complimenting him on his physique. I took my cellphone out of my pocket and rang Flavio Guarnero, gave him the name of the bar and clicked off.

We looked on as Donatella slowly pushed her bags under the table towards Chiarenza with her feet. Then, after a couple of minutes, she got up, shouldered her crocodile-skin bag and asked Chiarenza if he would be so kind as to keep an eye on her baggage while she went to the toilet. He replied with a smile that lingered a long while on his face. Perhaps he was savouring in advance the moment he'd possess and torture the woman. Watching him, I realized he wasn't the slightest bit afraid and was no doubt planning to return from Japan quite soon. Perhaps he had tried to bring his departure forward as a mere matter of precaution, while waiting to discover who had eliminated Giachino. I told Max what was I thinking.

'I figure you're right,' he sighed. 'It's too late now.'

After about ten minutes Chiarenza began to check his watch and crane his neck to see if Donatella was on her way back over, looking on with interest as a group of police officers walked into the bar. When he realized they were heading his way he jumped out of his seat, but there was already a plain-clothes cop positioned behind him who quickly put his handgun to the back of his head. Then they handcuffed him and led him away while two of the officers collected the bags, including Donatella's. Her holdall contained the videos documenting the torturing and killing of Helena, Mariano Giraldi and Barbie Slave, plus the rope flower discovered in the hotel room from which Helena had been abducted. Our personal compliments to the Master.

EPILOGUE

Old Rossini was released from prison the following week, after the Guardia di Finanza had arrested a Bosnian as he was trying to cross the border with a bag full of cash. In exchange for a promise of exceptional leniency, the Bosnian had squealed, enabling the cops to arrest the entire gang that had done the security-van job.

Rossini came by the club the same evening he was released. There was a lot of hugging, then Beniamino suggested we went up to my flat so we could talk things over, away from any indiscreet ears. The moment he stepped over the threshold, he pulled a newspaper cutting out of his pocket. It carried the news of the Master of Knots' arrest and the uncovering of a vast illegal pornography network. Chiarenza had handed the investigators the names of his accomplices. Only one of them, Michele Narsi, had evaded capture. The investigation promised to be sensational and the more lurid aspects of the case had aroused considerable press interest.

'What the fuck does this mean?' he asked, struggling to control his anger.

I cleared my throat, trying to find the right tone of voice. 'You weren't around,' I replied. 'We had to make do.'

Max supplied a detailed account of events while Rossini

listened and shook his head. 'I can't believe it,' he snorted finally. 'You went to a cop and a hooker for help in putting that piece of shit in prison.'

'He was on the point of skipping the country.'

'He deserved to die.'

'He won't have a great time behind bars either.'

'By the way,' Max asked. 'How have these last couple of weeks been?'

Beniamino stared at him like he was crazy. Then he slapped his hand down hard on the table. 'It says here that the Master of Knots was convinced that the murder of Giachino had nothing to do with his gang's activities,' he yelled. 'That bastard would have come back from Japan and we would have been able to resolve this in our own way.'

'It's true,' I admitted. 'We realized that too late. We rushed things. Just like you did when you whacked that moron Giachino. The fact is, right from the start we were operating in a world about which we knew nothing and that's always how mistakes are made.'

Old Rossini got up, I noticed a new golden bracelet dangling from his left wrist: the scalp of Ugo, the cameraman. He must have bought it immediately after his release from prison.

'I'm going back to Sylvie's place,' he said, and left without saying goodbye, closing the door gently behind him.

'He's not in a great mood,' Fat Max remarked.

'He'll get over it,' I said. 'Try not to go on about prison so much, otherwise he'll get seriously pissed off.'

'All right, I'll keep my tongue on a leash. Shall we go back down to the club?'

'There's no rush. Besides, I want a word with you.'

'What about?'

'I've decided to offer you a partnership. A fifty per cent share.'

He looked at me in surprise. 'Thanks, but I've not got enough money to . . .'

'I don't want any money.'

'I don't get it. You're offering me a half-share in La Cuccia?'

'Including the headaches.'

'But, Marco, why?'

'We're friends. That's all.'

'I can't accept.'

'Yes, you can. This place is doing pretty nicely and you need some security too. In our line of work, you never know what can happen, so it's wise to have your arse covered.'

Max stared at me. 'That's not the only reason, is it?'

I lit a cigarette. 'No, it isn't. I'd like you to have the financial peace of mind to choose freely what to do with your life.'

'What are you saying?'

'In that hotel in Turin you said you weren't happy with your life.'

'The work we do rules out other choices.'

I shrugged. 'We'll stay friends in any case, and besides, to be honest, I envy you the fact that you still have dreams.'

Max remained silent for a long while. 'I don't know what to say.'

'Then don't waste your breath.'

He gave my shoulder a big squeeze and returned to the club. I calmly finished my cigarette, feeling satisfied. I'd done the right thing. Then I picked up my cellphone and called Virna. 'Do words still mean anything between us?'

'Maybe,' she replied.

I met her in a bar in the centre of town and found her more beautiful than usual. I said a couple of things of no importance, then drank my glass of Calvados straight down and began to talk. I told her who I really was and why I'd chosen the work I did. Why it was so essential to me to go stirring up shit and playing hide and seek with gangsters, cops and magistrates, how it gave some meaning to my life. I opened up in a way I had never done with anybody, and when I finished I looked her in the eye.

'The worst of the heat's over,' she said simply. 'At last we can breathe again.'

She smiled and stroked the back of my hand with a finger. She always did that when she wanted to make love.